GIRL-CRAZY

Jerry was all set for the best summer of his life. It seemed a sure thing when Ken suggested they take a job out west at the Lost River Dude Ranch.

Maybe it *would* be a good idea to get out of the city, Jerry thought, into some fresh air, and away from thinking about girls all the time. A new adventure. How could they miss?

How could Jerry guess that their vacation would end in near-tragedy, and that his best friend would begin to hate him — all because of a promise he couldn't keep, a faith he didn't have, and a girl he couldn't resist?

It would take a miracle to save Jerry's summer, and Jerry didn't believe in miracles — until that summer changed his life.

Jerry's Summer

Ed Groenhoff

David C. Cook Publishing Co.
ELGIN, ILLINOIS—WESTON, ONTARIO

David C. Cook Publishing Co., Elgin, IL 60120
Printed in the United States of America
Library of Congress Catalog Number: 75-18988
ISBN: 0-912692-83-9

To Gordy

CONTENTS

1

A Job for the Summer

THE RED LIGHT ON THE DASH indicated that the motor was beginning to overheat.

"If that temperature gauge knows what it's talking about, we'd better stop," Jerry said.

"Yeah," Ken answered, glancing at the dash.

Ken pulled the '63 Chev into the small parking area, set the emergency brake, and put the car in neutral.

Another car might have been able to get to the top without overheating, but Ken's car had several things going against it. Its speedometer had turned over once, it had just gone nonstop for more than a thousand miles, and it was overloaded. The back seat and trunk were crammed with clothes, radios, record players, and anything else two boys needed, or thought they needed, for three months of work in the mountains.

When the red light went out again Ken shut off the motor, and the boys went over to the rocky ledge to get a better view of the valley below. They stood silently for a few minutes, taking in the spectacular view.

From where they stood they could look down into a V-shaped valley. Through the open end they could see the foothills they had just driven across. Beyond the hills, in the distance, were the Great Plains. In the opposite direction, the valley came to an abrupt halt against the main range of the Rockies. Towering above that end were the high, jagged, snow-covered peaks which make up the continental divide. The snow, glistening in the sunlight, made the peaks stand out in sharp contrast to the blue Colorado sky.

Some distance below the snow was the timberline where the dark green pine trees began to cover the slopes. At lower elevations and on the valley floor the pines gave way to the yellowish-green aspen. In the bottom of the valley a creek wandered in and out of the aspen and across some open grass areas.

"There it is." Ken pointed toward the far end of the valley.

"Nothing but trees." Jerry shook his head.

"See that clearing at the other end of the valley? It's directly below the highest peak."

"Well, maybe. You must have been nuts about carrots to have developed such sharp eyes."

"It's practice, Flatlander," Ken said. "Once you've been here awhile you'll learn to spot the clearings. This is the only road leading into the valley. We go up for another couple of miles, then we begin to wind down into the valley. From where we turn off the main road it's still about five miles to the ranch. They don't call it Lost River Ranch for nothing."

"Just so we get there — and fast," Jerry said. "Frankly, I've had it! After sitting in that crate for two days, I'm not sure I'll ever sit again."

"It got us here, didn't it?" Ken said, grinning.

"At the cost of a few years of my life."

This was to be Jerry's first year at Lost River Ranch, but Ken's second. Ken had first heard about the ranch from Carl Johnson, a friend of his father, who had come to Chicago on a business trip and stayed in their home for a couple of days. While he was there he talked about the dude ranch he operated near Aspen Park, Colorado, and left some brochures describing it.

Lost River Ranch, according to the brochure, offered "a vacation for the whole family." Each family lived in a separate cabin, but meals were served in the central dining room. Activities were provided for the family, including swimming, horseback riding, hiking, and overnights. The brochure described the work crew as "courteous, friendly, and helpful."

When Ken began to think about a summer job,

he remembered the ranch, and wrote to Mr. Johnson. After a few exchanges of letters, he was all set for a summer of work in the Rockies. The experience had been even greater than he had anticipated, so when Carl asked him to return the following summer, he accepted immediately.

When Ken returned home that fall he met Jerry. The Fredricksons had moved into the house next to the Langs during the summer. It was on Ken's first evening home, while he was in the backyard shaking out his sleeping bag, that Jerry hopped over the hedge separating their yards and introduced himself. From then on the two were constant companions, even though Ken was a year older than Jerry.

If opposites attract, then the secret to Ken and Jerry's friendship must have been in their differences. Ken was tall and slender with dark hair. Jerry, on the other hand, was only 5 feet 7, and he had given up ever getting any taller. He had light blond hair that fell across his forehead, sometimes hiding his bright blue eyes.

Ken was usually serious, and his face was often expressionless. But Jerry's mouth was naturally shaped into a smile. This was frequently a problem for him, because people never knew when he was serious and when he was joking.

Jerry had well-developed muscles, and his whole body gave evidence of spending many hours in the pool practicing for the swimming team. Ken had long, thin arms and legs which often embarrassed him on the beach, but which he used to become top scorer on the varsity basketball team during his junior year.

Ken was well enough liked, but had only a few really close friends. There was something about his height and actions that commanded respect. Everyone knew where he stood on moral and ethical issues. Because of their respect, his classmates often elected him to places of leadership. Although he had dated a few girls, Ken didn't go out of his way to make girl friends. But wherever Jerry was, there were girls — lots of them. He loved every second of the attention he got, and made the most of it.

Ken and Jerry were different in another way — a way which Jerry found most perplexing. Every time he suggested to Ken that they go someplace it seemed that Ken was either going to a youth meeting, Bible club, or another church service.

Jerry had only been in church a few times in his life, and that was for a couple of weddings, and his grandpa's funeral. Once his folks had decided to take the whole family to a Christmas service, but it hadn't made much of an impression on Jerry.

So he was puzzled about Ken's genuine interest in church. He could understand someone going on Sunday morning — lots of his friends did that — but Ken generally went on Sunday night too, plus all the church activities during the week.

The boys didn't discuss it until one day when Ken was elected president of the newly formed Bible club at school. On the way home that night Jerry asked, "Say, what's with this Bible club bit?"

"It's easier to show than to explain," Ken replied. "How about coming Thursday after school and finding out for yourself?"

"Don't know what I'm getting into, but I guess that's a fair enough answer," Jerry replied.

So on Thursday Jerry was there. He liked the kids, especially a couple of the sharp girls, and he listened to everything. The following Thursday he came again without an invitation.

After the third meeting, Jerry went home with Ken. As they sat and talked in Ken's room, he had a lot of questions. He asked about God, the Bible, and what the kids meant when they testified about being "saved."

Ken admitted he didn't know the answers to some of his questions, but he tried to explain what it meant to become a Christian. He told Jerry about when he had accepted Christ as his personal Savior, and what Christ had meant to him since that time. Jerry seemed eager to hear more, but the telephone rang, and it was his mother calling to say that dinner was ready.

That night Ken prayed for Jerry, and asked God to help him introduce Jerry to Jesus Christ.

He lay awake a long time that night thinking about what he had said, and what he should have said. Although he had been going to church all his life, he realized that this was the first time he had really talked to anyone personally about Christ. The excitement of it kept him awake.

In the weeks that followed, it seemed there was never the same kind of opportunity to talk to Jerry. When Ken heard through some of his friends that Carl was looking for a lifeguard for the summer, he immediately thought of Jerry. It would be fun to have his best friend along and maybe this could be his opportunity to tell Jerry more about Christ.

Ken had been talking about Lost River Ranch all winter, so when he mentioned the possibility of working there, Jerry was ready to go. They discussed it with his parents, who were happy to see him find a summer job. Ken wrote to Carl recommending Jerry, and within a few days Jerry got a letter from Carl, asking him to come out for the summer.

As soon as school was out, Jerry and Ken packed Ken's car and headed west. Ken was a senior and had graduated, so his last few weeks had been rather hectic. His parents wanted him to rest a few days before leaving, but to get to the ranch for opening day they had to leave the morning following graduation.

As they stood now looking over the valley,

Ken whispered a little prayer. "Lord, please make that valley the place where Jerry finds You."

2

Lost River Ranch

By the time the '63 Chev had reached the side road leading down into the valley, Ken had shifted into low, and the radiator was again near the boiling point. But as soon as he turned off the main road it was all downhill and once again the light went out.

Ken leaned back in his seat and exclaimed, "Whew! I really wasn't sure she'd make it."

"Now you tell me!" Jerry laughed.

"Even mothers have occasional doubts about their children, you know."

"Some mothers should."

"I have a feeling I should ignore that remark." Then, giving a sweep of his hand, Ken said, "Isn't this the greatest?"

"I'll admit that it's more scenic than north Chicago," Jerry said, "except for the females."

"Aw, come off it," Ken said. "We've only been gone from home two days, and already you're missing your girls. I can see this is going to be a long, dry summer."

"Now don't tell me that no girls ever find their way into this valley. What about those pictures you showed me from last summer?"

"Sure, some girls do come along with their parents as guests. But just remember, they're guests, and you're staff. That means you can look, but you can't touch."

"I hate it already." Jerry pretended to pout.

"Don't I remember you promising a little red-head just two days ago that you would think about her all summer?"

"Did I say that?"

"You sure did. In fact, I just may feel it is my brotherly duty to write to Ann once in awhile to report on your conduct."

"You wouldn't spoil a buddy's summer like that, would you?" Then without waiting for an answer, he said, "OK, wise guy, where's the ranch?"

"Just about a thousand more aspens and we'll be there. Why don't you count them. It'll keep your mind off girls."

"Finally," Jerry exclaimed as they rounded the last corner and the gates of the ranch came into view.

The gateway was framed with a high post on

each side of the gate and a plank across the top on which the name, Lost River Ranch, had been painted. Looking past the gate the boys could see the dining hall to the right. It was a long log building with a wide porch facing east. It was built that way so that after breakfast the guests could sit in the big chairs, read their morning papers, and get the full benefit of the warm morning sun.

Behind the dining hall a little stream came out of the mountains and ran past the entrance gate to become part of Lost River. A foot bridge over the stream led to a series of cabins stacked in several tiers along the hillside. Each cabin also had a porch facing east. Early risers could watch the sun come up over the foothills and see the crew preparing for the day's activities.

To the left of the lane was the manager's house, and some distance behind it was a large barn and corral where the riding horses were kept. In the middle of the ranch, directly in front of the main entrance, was a large open pavilion. This was used for evening gatherings. Here guests huddled around the fireplace after dark and exchanged stories about their hometowns. And occasionally staff members put on skits for the guests. On rainy days it was used as a recreation area. Ping-Pong tables were stacked at one end, and shuffle-board lanes were painted on the concrete floor.

Behind the pavilion, and also in the center of

the ranch, was the pool. It was far from an olympic-size pool, but it did have a deep end and was equipped with both low and high diving boards. Separate from the main pool, but within the same fenced-in area, was a wading pool for the children. Jerry looked for the pool immediately, as that was to be his domain for the next three months.

And behind all of this were the mountains. To the south and west were the high peaks of the main range, and to the east were the foothills. Even one of the foothills rose to more than 10,000 feet, and it was the goal of many guests to climb Prophet's Peak at least once during their stay at Lost River Ranch.

Ken brought the car to a stop in front of the dining hall. By the time the boys got out of the car, another boy, about Jerry's height, but with dark red hair, jumped up from one of the big chairs, letting the book he was reading drop to the floor. He yelled, "Ken! We thought you'd never get here." Then over his shoulder he called, "Hey, Jan. Come out and see what just dropped in from the big city."

Ken ran up the steps and grabbed the redhead's hand and shook it vigorously. "Dick! Man, it's good . . ."

Just then the screen door of the dining hall opened and a girl, about 5 foot 3 with long blonde hair, ran and threw her arms around Ken. "Welcome home! I was so glad when Daddy said you would be here again this summer."

"Hi, Jan." Ken gave her an awkward hug.

By this time Jerry was also on the porch. "Is this the work you were talking about?" he asked.

"Oh, excuse me, Jerry. This is Jan. Jan Johnson. She lives here. Carl's daughter, you know."

"Hello, Jerry," Jan said, moving over toward him.

Jerry put out his hand, but she ignored it. "A friend of Ken's is a friend of mine," she said, and gave Jerry a big hug.

"Wow! I like the way you pick your friends," Jerry said to Ken.

"And this is Dick Griffith," Ken continued. "He's in charge of recreation. You know, he sets up the horseshoe stakes for the old men, and gets out the checker boards for the old ladies."

"And don't forget holding the skipping rope for the little girls," Dick added.

"Hi, Dick. I'm Jerry," he said, extending his hand.

"Welcome to the ranch."

"Where's Carl?" Ken asked.

"He's up in Cabin Four repairing a leaky faucet in the bathroom," Dick answered. "He told us to tell you to come up there."

"Come on, Jerry," Ken said. "I want you to meet the boss."

"Good-bye, Jerry," Jan said. "I can tell this is going to be the best summer ever."

Jerry felt himself blushing a little.

"Don't believe a word she says. She tells that to all the fellows." Ken motioned for Jerry to follow him.

"Be fair, Ken," Jan said. "Give him a fair chance to make up his own mind about me."

"Look. I hereby appoint myself a committee of one to protect him from you."

"Hey, don't I get to say anything about it?" Jerry asked.

"Right now, no." This time Ken took him by the arm. "Come on, let's go see Carl."

Jerry followed Ken around the dining hall, across the footbridge, and up along the row of cabins that lined the ridge overlooking the ranch. They walked until they came to Cabin Four.

"Hey, Carl. We're here." Ken called.

A middle-aged man with a round smiling face and a receding hairline stuck his head out of the bathroom door. "Glad to see you made it. Be right with you."

Carl put down his wrenches and came out of the bathroom wiping his hands on his jeans. He shook hands with Ken. "Welcome again," he said. "And I presume this is your friend, Jerry."

"That's right," Ken said. "Jerry, this is Mr. Johnson. Just call him Carl. We all do."

"Yes," Carl said, "we all get to know one another very well around here. By the end of the summer you'll feel like you're part of a big family. We even have a few family arguments, don't we, Ken?"

" 'Fraid so," Ken said. "But we get over them."

"Why don't you boys go over and get settled. We'll be having dinner about 5:30. After dinner I want to talk to the whole staff about the work ahead. The guests will start coming the day after tomorrow, so that means we have lots of work to do before then."

"Where do you want us this year?" Ken asked.

"Why don't you two take the north end of the bunkhouse. Dick has his things in the south side."

Ken and Jerry went back and moved the car over by a cabin which stood behind and a little above the manager's house. It was a double cabin with a door at each end. In the north part there were two single beds, two chests of drawers and two desks. There was one large closet, and a bathroom with shower, sink, and stool.

After they had put their things away, and the car was empty, Jerry fell back on his bed. "Wow, this is going to feel great tonight."

Ken sat down on the bed across from Jerry. "Not having gone to bed last night is only part of your problem," Ken explained. "It takes a few days to get used to this altitude. Last year all I wanted to do the first week was sleep."

Ken lay back on his bed and both were silent for a few minutes. Finally Jerry spoke.

"Ken."

"Yeah."

"That Jan is something, isn't she?"

"Here we go again," Ken said. "Are girls all you think about?"

"You didn't answer my question," Jerry insisted.

Ken hesitated for a moment. "Yes. Yes, she is. But I warn you, she's different. You never know where you are with her. One day she's as warm as a kitten, and the next day she acts like she doesn't know you."

"Is she a Christian?"

Ken sat up and leaned on his elbow so that he could look at Jerry. "Yes, I suppose so. Why?"

"Nothing. Just wondering."

They were silent again and Ken lay back down.

"You like her, don't you, Ken?"

Ken didn't answer right away, and it was Jerry's turn to sit up so he could look at Ken.

Ken turned so that he could look squarely at Jerry and said, "Jerry, to be honest, she's the only girl I have ever really liked."

"I thought so."

"How could you tell?" Ken asked.

"Experience, I suppose."

"So give with the advice, Mr. Experience."

"Thanks, but no thanks. You're on your own, buddy, but good luck."

"I'll need it."

Both boys lay staring at the ceiling until it was time to go to dinner.

3

Jerry's Initiation

Sorry, MEN," Carl said, shaking the beds. "We've got a lot to do before the guests arrive tomorrow."

Jerry stretched and opened his eyes.

"Good morning, I think," he mumbled.

"Sure, it's a good morning," Carl said. "Every morning is a good morning in Colorado. It may rain before night, but every morning is beautiful. That's why everybody gets up early out here."

"Everybody but city kids and tourists." Ken's voice came from beneath his covers.

"Well, you're not tourists, and for the next three months you're not city kids, so up and at 'em." Carl started to leave.

"OK, we'll be there," Ken said, pulling the covers from his head. "But you've got to give us a little time to adjust to this schedule."

"I must not have had any trouble with you last summer, or I wouldn't have hired you again." Carl laughed and went out the door.

Ken sat up on the edge of his bed and looked over at Jerry. "OK, if I can get up, you can, too." Then Ken's face brightened. "Besides, I wouldn't want you to miss your initiation day."

"Initiation day?" Jerry sat up in bed.

"Sure. All first-time staffers get initiated the night before the first guests arrive."

"I think I just decided to walk home."

"Think of the blisters."

"On second thought, I'll stay. But what's with this initiation bit?"

"You'll find out soon enough. Come on, let's go to breakfast. Forget shaving this morning. When the guests arrive we'll have to clip every whisker." He paused, then snapped his fingers. "Oops! I almost forgot that I'm dealing with a minor who doesn't need to shave every day."

"Would you believe every other day?"

Ken and Jerry dressed and went to the dining hall. Carl, Jan, and Dick were already there, and Mrs. Johnson had breakfast awaiting them.

They sat down around a large table in the staff dining room which was just off the kitchen. Carl bowed his head and gave thanks for the food. He thanked the Lord for bringing the staff together again this year, and prayed for another good year. Then they ate. There was a big platter of pancakes, plenty of butter and syrup, and a plate heaped with country sausage patties.

Following breakfast Carl assigned the work for the day. Ken and Dick were to use the truck to move the lawn furniture out of the barn and distribute it in front of each cabin, and at other places on the grounds. Jan and Patty Stevens, a girl from a neighboring ranch who came in each day to work, were to make the beds in the cabins and put clean linens in all the bathrooms. Jerry was to get the pool ready and filled with water.

Jerry went to his cabin and changed into his swim trunks and pulled an old sweatshirt over his head. The idea of being completely in charge of a pool was exciting to him. He had practically lived at the pool every summer, but this was his first chance to have complete responsibility for one.

There was plenty of work to do, and by noon he was already beginning to feel some aching muscles. At lunch he said to Ken, "Man, this is even harder than going to school. I thought I was in pretty good shape, but I've got aches in muscles I didn't even know I had."

Ken laughed and said, "You'll survive. Like I told you last night, it takes a few days to get adjusted to this altitude. We're between nine and ten thousand feet. There's a lot less oxygen for your lungs to breathe. Don't be surprised if you have to use smelling salts on guests when they first try to swim up here."

"Thanks for warning me," Jerry replied. "Of course, it will all depend upon the age and sex of the guest as to how much attention I give."

"Just remember, it's the older ones who pay the bills."

Most of the assigned work was done by about 4 p.m., so Carl told the boys to knock off work and get cleaned up. No one had said a word about initiation during the day, so Jerry was beginning to think they had forgotten about it. He got his first hint that it was still on when he said to Ken, "Well, I had better shower and shave before dinner."

Ken replied, "Go ahead if you'll feel better, but you'll probably have to do it again before the night is over."

"And just what do you mean by that?"

"Forget that I said anything," Ken called from the shower. He turned the water on full blast so Jerry couldn't have a chance to ask any more questions.

Jerry kicked off his shoes and threw himself on his bed. He would have to wait until Ken finished using the shower, so he would just rest a few minutes.

"Your turn," Ken called. When he didn't hear any response he opened the bathroom door and looked out. Jerry was sound asleep. Ken pulled a towel around himself and came over to the bed with a wet washcloth.

"Get up, lazy." He squeezed some water from the cloth on Jerry's face.

Jerry blinked and sputtered, "Why didn't you tell me you were through?"

"I did."

"You did not."

"I sure did, and you were sound asleep."

"Maybe a shower will wake me up."

After they had showered and shaved, Jerry was about to put on a pair of dress slacks when Ken said, "Save those for church. You're on a ranch now, and here you wear jeans and boots for everything. They even bury you in them here in the West."

"Cheery thought."

They went to the dining hall and ate dinner. Once again the staff ate in the special room, and already a sense of togetherness was developing. Patty stayed for dinner, so it was Jerry's first opportunity to get acquainted with her. After dinner they all sat around and talked. Then it was Ken who asked, "Isn't it about time we show our tenderfoot around the community?"

"For some reason I don't think I want to go," Jerry said.

"Now you wouldn't want to work here without knowing the community, would you?" Ken asked.

"What if a guest asked you about it?" Patty said.

"And what if some guest got lost? You

31

wouldn't know where to find him," Jan added.

"Come on, everybody," Ken called as he started out of the door.

They all piled into the open jeep. Ken and Dick kept Jerry between them in the front to discourage any attempt to leave the group, and Jan and Patty got in the back seat. Ken drove down the lane and out to the road that Jerry and Ken had come down the day before. Before they got to the main road they turned off on a trail that was just a clearing about eight feet wide with two wheel tracks running through it.

"This is a road?" Jerry asked.

"Relax. It gets a lot worse," Ken replied.

"Somebody must have forgotten to pay his taxes."

They drove on for several miles. At one point they stopped along a little ledge and everyone got out. The sun was just going down behind Long's Peak, and it cast long shadows across the valley. From where they stood they could see the buildings of the ranch nestled in the aspen.

"Remember our picnic here last year?" Jan asked.

"I don't remember any picnic," Dick said.

"You weren't invited!" Ken replied.

"So that's where you two were when Carl looked all over for you," Dick said.

"Keep talking," Jerry said. "I'm learning something."

"You've heard too much already," Ken replied. "Come on everyone, Jerry hasn't seen all the area yet."

As they drove on, the road became rougher. By now it was just an old logging trail. Once they had to stop the jeep and move a fallen branch. Another time they had to stop, back up, and make a run for a little stream so that they could get through it without getting stuck. As it became darker Ken turned on the headlights, and once they saw a deer run across the trail ahead. They came to several forks in the road, but each time Ken selected a fork without hesitation. He had obviously been over these roads before.

They finally came to a little clearing with a stream running through it. Ken stopped the jeep. "I think we had better examine the trail ahead to see if the jeep can make it," he said. "Jerry, why don't you run ahead and see if the jeep can cross that stream? You try it, and if you can jump it, the jeep can surely make it."

By this time Jerry was beginning to think that his initiation was merely a ride in the woods at night, so he didn't suspect anything. He got out and walked ten yards ahead. It was dark enough now that he had to strain his eyes to see the stream they were talking about. He carefully worked his way to the edge and then jumped over. When he made it, he called back, "It's OK. See, I made it."

"That's fine," Ken called. "We'll be waiting for you at the dining hall."

With that he started the motor and whirled the jeep around. Before Jerry could jump back across the stream they were already headed down the trail.

"Bye, bye, Jerry," Jan called. "We'll be waiting for you."

So this was it, he thought to himself. If only he had paid more attention to the directions. He stood there for a minute and looked around. He could pick out Long's Peak against the faint glow of the sunset. This meant that he would have to go in the general direction of the peak to get back home. He knew that he was on the opposite side of the valley, so the ranch had to be somewhere in between.

He thought of following the road back, but knew he would never remember all the forks. He finally decided to try a shorter route and began picking his way carefully over the rocks and boulders. He walked on for some distance without seeing anything that looked like a path. He tried to listen for some sounds from the ranch. Once he thought he heard the jeep coming closer again, but apart from that there was only silence.

Jerry never knew that the night could be so still. After living in the city, the stillness of it was almost smothering. He could hear himself breathe, and that was a little frightening.

34

He walked on farther. The only clue he had that he was headed in the right direction was the sensation of going down rather than up. After going a short distance, Jerry found a small clearing and sat down.

By now the last pink was gone from the west, and the sky was filled with stars. Jerry lay back and looked up. It seemed that the tall pine trees around him reached up until they almost touched the stars. He had never seen them look so close. A line from a song he had heard at Bible Club came to his mind. "In the stars His handiwork I see."

"There must be a God to have made all of that," he said to himself. His voice sounded strange in the stillness.

He closed his eyes for a moment, and then he found himself saying, "I don't know who You are, or where You are, but I believe You're there. And God, I want to get to know You better."

A warm feeling came over him. He had never felt this way before. Maybe it was just that he was tired — very, very tired.

Ken, Dick, and the girls sat down on the porch of the dining hall. "I'll bet Jerry hates us right now," Dick said.

"That's really a pretty mean trick," Jan said.

"Remember, you did it to me last year," Ken said. "I got back all right."

35

"Well, it really isn't very far," Patty said.

"But you sure don't know that when you're out there," Ken replied. "After all that driving you think you're a thousand miles away."

"He should be here in about half an hour," Jan said. "Let's make the popcorn and have it ready when he comes."

They all went inside. Carl had built a staff lounge in the basement of the dining hall. It contained a little kitchenette, and was furnished with some large soft chairs, a few small tables, and a television set.

Jan and Ken got out the ingredients to make the popcorn, and Patty and Dick turned on the TV.

When the popcorn was all made Jan looked at her watch and said, "Shouldn't he be here by now?"

"How long has it been?" Ken asked.

"It's been nearly three-quarters of an hour."

"You sure are worried about him. He'll be here any minute," Ken replied.

But after a full hour, Jerry still wasn't there. The popcorn was getting cold, so they began to eat it.

"I'm beginning to get worried," Jan said. "Don't you think we should go look for him?"

"I can't imagine how he could get lost," Ken said. "We left him only about a half mile from here."

"That's just the point. He was so close that he should be here by now."

Dick got up and turned off the TV. "I'm beginning to wonder myself. Let's go out and take a look."

"I'll go to the bunkhouse and get a couple of flashlights," Ken said.

"Think I'll go along and get a jacket," Dick said.

"And we'll get some sweaters and meet you here in a few minutes," Jan said.

The four started out, each couple carrying a flashlight. They went up the ridge and in the general direction of where they had left Jerry earlier.

They took turns calling, but there was no answer. Finally, they got to the place where they had let him out of the jeep, and they still hadn't seen him.

"Now I'm really worried," Jan said. "You guys should be ashamed of yourselves doing this to Jerry on his first night here. You could have at least waited until he got his directions straight."

"You guys?" Ken said. "Remember, you were in on it too."

"No use arguing who started it," Dick said. "We're all in it, and we've got to find him."

"Let's spread out and see if we can see any footprints," Ken said.

"But there are only two flashlights," Dick said.

"Naturally. You didn't want to be alone out here, did you?" Ken replied.

"Never thought of that."

"I'll bet you didn't."

Each couple started out in separate directions. They had only gone a little way when Ken called, "Pat, Dick, come here."

"What happened?" Dick called.

"Just come here. You'll see." Ken answered.

When the four were all together, Ken turned on his flashlight.

There was Jerry.

"Would you believe it? Sound asleep," Ken said.

"That's not even playing fair," Dick said.

"What . . . what?" Jerry began to wake up.

"Good morning," Jan said. "You just slept through your initiation."

"Come on, gang, let's go eat our popcorn." Ken sounded disgusted.

4

The Girl from Wisconsin

On Sunday morning Mr. and Mrs. Johnson went to an 8:30 a.m. service at a little community church in Aspen Park. Jan and Ken went with them, but Jerry and Dick slept in. When they came home from church, Mrs. Johnson served an early dinner so that everyone would be available to help when the guests began to arrive.

Carl reported to the staff that all 15 cabins were rented for the week, and that he was expecting 56 guests, ranging in age from a few months to a retired couple in their 70's.

Following dinner Ken, Jerry, Dick, Jan, and Patty all went to the office, an addition built on the side of the manager's house, to wait for the guests. It was about noon when the first car arrived.

The family was from Texas. There was a

mother, father, a ten-year-old girl, and an eight-year-old boy. Ken volunteered to show them to their cabin. While the parents drove the car to the cabin, the boy decided to walk with Ken. As they passed the corral he threw rocks at the horses, and when Ken stopped him from doing that, he began to throw rocks at Ken. By the time they got to the cabin, he had succeeded in knocking off Ken's hat.

"Beware of that little monster," Ken warned when he got back to the office. "This could be a long week."

"Two weeks," corrected Carl.

"You mean we gotta put up with him for two weeks?"

"I'm afraid so," replied Carl.

"I hope we have some windows left when he leaves," Ken said.

Just then a car with Wisconsin license plates pulled in.

"It's your turn to show them around," Ken said, pointing to Jerry.

"Thanks loads," Jerry said as he got up from his chair. "I'll remember your kindness to me." Then, after looking out the door, he exclaimed, "Yeah! I know I'll remember your kindness to me."

"Oh, no," Ken said. "There's only one thing that can make Jerry light up like that — a female. I get the mean little brat, and I give him the girl. Oh, well," he shrugged his shoulders, "you win a few, lose a lot."

"Now it isn't all that bad, is it?" Jan came over and sat down by Ken. "After all, you still have the two of us." She pointed to herself and Patty.

"In that case, I'll just have to make do with what I've got," Ken said.

"Thanks a lot," Jan replied.

Meanwhile Jerry had gotten the names of the guests and had come in for cabin assignment and keys. "This could be a great week," he said excitedly.

"Oh, boy," Jan said. "We should have left him in the woods last night."

"With someone like that around here I may even thank you for showing me the woods last night," Jerry said.

"Now, remember . . . ," Ken began.

"I know, I know," Jerry interrupted. "She's a guest and I'm on staff. Well, you can't stop me from looking."

Dick, who had been quiet through all of this, got up from his chair. "With a sales talk like that, I've got to see the product," he said.

"You too," Patty said. "You just can't trust a man."

Carl took the name and gave Jerry the keys to Cabin Five. When Jerry started out of the door, Ken and Dick both started to follow him.

"Hey, look guys, you'll get your turn. This one is mine," Jerry said.

"We'll remind him of that when something better comes along," Ken said to Dick.

When Jerry got back to the car he said to the driver, "If you would like to drive up to Cabin Five, I'll be there in a minute with the key."

A girl's voice from the back seat said, "Mind if I walk with you? I'm tired of sitting in this hot car."

"No, not at all." Jerry turned on his sharpest smile.

The door opened, and what Jerry saw made him blink. He could feel the eyes of the staff watching from the office. Out of the car stepped a girl in a two-piece sunsuit. She was about his height with shoulder-length platinum blonde hair. The car drove off, and Jerry and the girl started to walk.

"What's your name?" she asked.

"Jerry. Jerry Fredrickson. What's yours?"

"Sue Kelly. I really didn't want to come on this trip. I've been going on vacations with my parents all my life, and this year I thought I was old enough to go somewhere by myself. You think a 16-year-old is old enough to have a separate vacation, don't you?"

"Yes . . . I guess so. I really never thought about it before."

"Well, I have. I wanted to go with some other

kids to a cabin in Minnesota, but my parents are so prudish. They said I was too young, and that I would have to go with them! I don't know what they thought we would do up there!" She threw her head back, causing her hair to drop back behind her shoulders.

"I'm sorry," Jerry said. He didn't know why he said it, but he couldn't think of anything else to say at the moment.

"Like I said," she continued, "I didn't want to come, but they made me. Now that I see what they've got working here, it may not be so bad after all."

Jerry felt his face turning red. "Thanks . . . I think."

"What do you do around here?" Sue asked.

"Well, just about anything that needs to be done, but mostly, I'm in charge of the swimming pool."

"Ooh, a lifeguard. I thought you had to use those muscles for something like that. I'll be at the pool every minute it's open."

Jerry was glad they had arrived at her cabin, because he was beginning to feel a bit uncomfortable. He had been rushed before, but never like this. He unlocked the cabin and helped the family unload. Sue followed him every trip from the cabin to the car, but never offered to pick up anything herself. Finally, when they were all unloaded, he said, "If you want anything else, just let us know. Dinner will be served at 5:30 this evening."

"Where are you going now?" Sue asked.

"Back to the office."

"Can I come too?"

"I think you'd better wait. We've got other guests to help, and I'm not sure my friends would do any more work if you showed up."

"You mean there are more like you?" Sue giggled.

When Jerry got back to the office, Ken and Dick were waiting by the door.

"Well, how was it?" Dick asked.

"As Ken said before, these could be two mighty long weeks," Jerry answered.

"Listen to the kid," Ken said. "He sounds as if he didn't like it."

"Look, fellows, believe me, she's too fast for me. Just give me simple little old Ann back in Chicago."

"Somebody should have told you that you're not in Chicago, you're in the wild, wild West," Dick said.

"But she's not out to play cowboys and Indians," Jerry answered.

Another car interrupted their discussion.

For the next few hours all three boys were busy getting the guests settled. Each time Jerry went by Cabin Five, Sue would come out and make some remark, but he always excused himself by saying that other guests were waiting. He didn't know what he was going to do when that excuse was no longer true.

By 4 p.m. all the guests were settled, and the fellows used the pickup to get some wood for the fireplace in the pavilion. Supper was served at 5:30, and Carl announced to the guests that there would be a get-acquainted time in the pavilion beginning at 7:30 p.m.

At these get-acquainted sessions Carl would explain the facilities of the ranch, and introduce the staff. He would have each of the guests introduce himself and tell a little about his hometown. The evening would end with a sing-along led by Ken and Dick with their guitars.

Sue lived up to Jerry's predictions all week. When he would go to the corral in the morning to help get the horses saddled, she would be there watching, and in the afternoon she would be waiting by the gate for him to open the pool. Once she was in the pool she would do everything possible to attract his attention and try to get him to come in the water with her. When that didn't work she would sit on the edge and talk.

One afternoon, after the pool closed, Jerry went back to the bunkhouse to change clothes. Ken was lying on his bunk when Jerry came in.

"Why me, why me?" Jerry asked.

"Because you have so much sex appeal," Ken said.

45

"I wish I had studied karate instead of swimming. Look, be a pal, take her for a ride. Do something . . . anything, just to give me a few minutes of peace."

"That's a sad story," Ken teased. "And you're the one who asked me if any girls ever came to Lost River Ranch. Remember?"

"Wow, was I naive. They not only come, they come on strong."

By Friday Jerry's patience had run out. He decided that one more problem with Sue and he was going to tell her off, even if he got fired for it. He didn't have long to wait before he had his opportunity.

He had just started to saddle the horses when he heard that familiar voice behind him.

"Jerry, isn't this your day off?"

"Yes, it is, but how did you know?" Jerry asked without looking up.

"Oh, I saw the schedule." Sue jumped up and sat down on the top rail so that she could look at him.

Jerry stopped and looked up. He put his hands on his hips, tipped his hat back, and said, "You mean to tell me that you've been snooping on Carl's desk?"

"Oh, that makes it sound as if I did something awful. Let's just say that I happened to be in the office, and I happened to see the schedule."

"Well, whatever you call it, you were in some-

46

thing that was none of your business."

"I thought you would be flattered that some-one was that concerned about you."

"If you were really concerned about me, you would just leave me alone so that I can do my job without being fired."

"But I thought your job was to keep the guests happy."

"Well, some guests demand an awful lot of attention."

"I could tell my folks to leave and not stay another week. How would Carl like that? Espe-cially when he found out that we weren't happy with the service."

"You wouldn't . . . on second thought, you would."

"Do I get to go with you on your afternoon off, or don't I?" She stared down at him.

"Look, I've got things to do. It's the only time I have to wash clothes, write letters, and get into town."

"And I could help you with all those things," she said.

Jerry was beginning to lose his patience. "All I want from you is for you to go get lost."

"If that's the way you feel about it, that's just what I'll do. I'll go into the mountains by myself and get lost, and then you'll have to come find me, or Carl will fire you."

"I'll take my chances."

All was quiet, and Jerry didn't dare look up. Finally, his curiosity got the best of him, and he raised his eyes. Sue was gone.

Sue didn't show up for lunch, and she wasn't at the pool that afternoon. When she didn't come to dinner, her parents contacted Carl.

5

A Narrow Escape

JERRY WENT INTO TOWN that afternoon to use the laundromat, and Jan substituted for him at the pool. He wanted to stay away from the ranch as long as possible, so he ate dinner in town before returning. When he finally arrived it was about 7 p.m., and Carl was waiting for him at the bunkhouse.

"Are you alone?" Carl asked.

"Sure. Why?"

"We were hoping that Sue was with you."

"Now, you wouldn't wish that on me, would you?" he answered with a laugh.

"I'm afraid this isn't a joke," Carl said. "No one has seen her since morning. Do you know anything about this?"

By this time Ken and Dick had joined the other two in the bunkhouse.

"All I know is that I talked to her this morning," Jerry answered, dumping his laundry on his bed. "She wanted to go with me this afternoon, and when I told her that she couldn't, she said something about going into the woods and getting lost . . ." Jerry thought for a moment. "That crazy girl. She wouldn't . . . on second thought, she would."

"A clear case of spurned love," Ken said, shaking his head.

"Aw, come off it," Jerry snapped. "You guys would have done the same thing."

"I can see it all now," Dick teased. "She will rush into the arms of her rescuer."

"Look, fellows," Carl interrupted. "This may seem funny to you, but it's getting dark and if she really is lost it's a serious matter. We've got to go look for her. Dick, you take the jeep and go up the old logging trail. Ken and Jerry, you start up toward Prophet's Peak. I'll take the car and go both ways on the main road and ask if anyone has seen her. She could have covered a lot of distance in a whole day."

By this time everyone at the ranch knew about Sue's disappearance. Most of the guests gathered in the pavilion to wait for further word. Mrs. Johnson made some extra coffee, and one of the guests kept the fireplace going. Each time someone would come back from the search, the whole group would go out to meet him, and when there was no new word they would go back to the pavilion to await the next person's return.

By about 10:30 all members of the search party were back at camp, and there were no clues as to Sue's whereabouts. It was getting rather chilly in the pavilion, so Carl suggested that everyone go into the dining hall. They were just entering the building when the telephone rang. Carl went to answer.

"Hello. Lost River Ranch. Yes . . . yes, we have a guest who answers to that description."

Everyone in the room stood motionless. All eyes were focused upon Carl. He was listening intently.

"Yes, thank you," he said. "We'll be right down." He hung up the receiver.

"Well, it seems that we have located Sue," he told the waiting group. "The police are holding her in Aspen Park."

Sue's parents gasped.

"They picked her up about a mile out of town a little while ago," Carl continued. "She appears to be unharmed, but is so hysterical that they haven't found out much. Apparently she had a rather frightening experience. Mr. and Mrs. Kelly, you had better come with me. The rest of you get some rest."

"Since I'm apparently the cause of this whole mess, don't you think I had better go, too?" Jerry asked.

"That's not a bad idea," Carl answered. "Then we can get the whole story straightened out."

When they arrived at the police station, Sue ran across the room and threw herself into her mother's arms and began to sob hysterically. The men stood around shuffling their feet awkwardly until Jerry decided to go sit down, and the others followed.

The police officer waited until Sue had quieted somewhat, and then he motioned for her to sit down too. When he finally had her attention, he said, "Now, Miss Kelly, if you can just tell us what happened, we can finish these reports, and you can go home and get some sleep."

In a voice that was just above a whisper, and broken occasionally by a sob, Sue told her story.

She had watched from the window of her cabin until she saw Jerry leave for town. Then, making sure that no one was watching, she walked down the lane and out to the main road. She planned to catch a ride into town and surprise him. She had gone only a short distance when a pickup truck carrying two men stopped. The driver, a middle-aged man with several days' growth of beard, asked her if she wanted a ride. His voice sounded as if he had been drinking, so Sue refused. Instead of driving on, the driver opened the door of the truck and got out. His companion did the same, and before she could run, they grabbed her and forced her into the cab.

52

With Sue in the seat between them, they drove up an old logging road to a little two-room cabin which seemed to be the home of one of the men. Both of them had been drinking heavily, and when they got to the cabin they started to drink again. They kept telling the frightened girl how long it had been since they had been visited by such a nice young girl, and how much they appreciated her visit. Then they would give big belly laughs and take some more drinks.

Eventually one of the men stumbled outdoors, and left the door open. She had waited for her opportunity, and when the other man turned his back, she darted out the open door. The man in the cabin called after her, and both men started running in an attempt to catch her, but by this time they were both so drunk that Sue was able to outdistance them easily.

She ran without stopping to the main road, and then fell exhausted into the ditch. She could hear loud shouting and cursing in the distance, but the men were never able to get as far as the road.

When she could no longer hear their voices, she crept into the nearby woods and remained there until dark. Her plan was to walk back to the ranch, but when she got on the road she couldn't remember which way to go. She was standing beside the road crying when the highway patrolman, on a routine cruise, spotted her.

"Then they didn't actually harm you in any way?" the officer asked.

"No, thank goodness. They were planning to. But I got out in time."

"And you would be able to identify the men if you were called upon to do so?"

"Yes, yes. I'll see those ugly faces in my mind for the rest of my life."

"I think that will be all for tonight, Miss Kelly," the officer said. Then, turning to the parents, he said, "I think you had better take her back to the ranch. We'll be contacting you soon. Are you staying there for a few days?"

"Yes," Mr. Kelly answered. "We'll be there all of next week if you need us."

Jerry had been listening to all of this, and he was arguing with himself. One minute he felt sorry for Sue, and guilty about not taking her with him, and the next minute he found himself thinking that it was good enough for her after all the grief she had given him.

When they all stood up to go, Sue realized for the first time that Jerry was in the group. She walked over to him and looked directly into his eyes.

"Jerry, I'm sorry about the way I've acted. I promise I won't cause you any more trouble from now on."

"Well . . . uh . . . ," Jerry stammered and looked around at the group. "Look, Sue, there's too many people here. Couldn't we just talk about it tomorrow at the pool?"

"OK, tomorrow." Sue smiled and reached out to touch his arm.

6

A Different Sort of Preacher

BESIDES HAVING ONE DAY OFF during the week, each crew member was free on Saturday evenings. On a normal Saturday, the staff got up about 5:30 a.m., and ate breakfast before any of the guests arrived at the dining hall. That way they could be ready to help anyone who wanted to check out immediately after breakfast.

Saturday was check-out day at the ranch, and except for a few who planned to stay on a second week, most of the guests would be gone by 10 a.m. As soon as a cabin was empty the crew would begin to clean it, getting it ready for the new guests who would arrive the next day.

Although it meant hard work, most of the crew looked forward to Saturday. It was the one day in which they could just be themselves. For one day they could forget pleasing the guests and just be a group of teenagers working together. The whole operation took on the air of a high school committee cleaning up after a school party. The singing, the nonsense talk, the sweat, and the fatigue all became a traditional part of Saturday afternoon. There were times when Carl had to remind them that there was still work to be done.

Generally, by 4 p.m. the cabins were cleaned, the linens changed, and everything was ready for the new guests. This meant that the crew was free to do whatever they wished as there were no planned activities for the guests on Saturday night. Often the crew was completely tired out by night, but a shower, some fresh clothes, and the thought of a free night made them forget the work of the day.

The only town within 30 miles was Aspen Park. It was a sleepy little mountain town during the winter, but it grew to about ten times its normal size during the height of the tourist season. Nearly every Saturday night the crew from the ranch would borrow Carl's jeep and go into Aspen Park. Hundreds of young people who worked in restaurants and resorts in the area would also be in town, so there was never a lack of activity in the summer.

"Ready?" Ken called above the noise of the motor.

"Be there in a minute," Jerry yelled back through the open window of the bunkhouse. "Go pick up Jan and Patty first, and by then I'll be dressed."

Ken gunned the motor a couple of times as an answer, and headed for the manager's cabin. He came to a halt in a cloud of dust in front of the door. Jan and Patty were waiting.

Jerry's preoccupation with Sue for two weeks had given Ken an opportunity to spend a lot of time with Jan. They often sat for several hours together on the porch after the day's work was done. Ken even arranged his day off so that it coincided with Jan's. The arrangements posed no problem because Carl liked Ken, and saw through his request immediately. Now, even though Sue had been gone for a week, Ken felt relatively secure in his relationship with Jan.

"Wow, going somewhere?" Ken whistled.

"Thank you, Mr. Lang," Jan said. "If you think we look that good, how about opening the door for us?"

"Sorry," Ken said. "Guess a month in the mountains has taken the gentleman out of me."

"You are implying that there was some before you came," Patty joked.

"Ladies, I assure you that back home I'm the model for all young men in the community," Ken said as he opened the door and took a low sweeping bow.

"Model for what?" Jan quipped as she stepped into the jeep.

"Just get in. You can stretch my good nature too far. You would hate to walk back home tonight."

"Where's Jerry?" Jan asked, looking into the back seat.

"And Dick?" Patty added as she climbed in.

"Dick is already in town and will meet us there. He went in with Carl. Jerry will be here in a minute. It takes him longer to get ready for his women," Ken said as he slipped into the driver's seat.

"He seems to do all right without much artificial help," Jan said. "Did you ever see anyone fall for a guy like that Sue Kelly did for Jerry?"

"Maybe he'll just stay home and eat his heart out tonight. I'm sure that's what Sue is doing." Patty laughed.

"If you think Jerry will lose sleep over Sue, you don't know him very well," Ken said. "I've been watching him operate all year at school, and I'll bet you ten to one that before this night is over he'll have some other girl chasing him."

"You sound worried," Jan said.

"What do you mean by that?" Ken asked.

"I could chase him pretty easy, you know."

"I know, and I'm worried," Ken admitted.

"Just so there isn't any trouble, I'll have Jerry sit back here with me," Patty said.

"Somebody call me?" Jerry said, coming around the corner.

"Get in Romeo, and let's get going," Ken said.

"Hey, what's with the Romeo bit?" Jerry asked. "I have a feeling that I was being talked about."

"It was all good," Patty said. "Now, get back here with me, and at least look like you're enjoying it."

"A back seat, a female . . . and me. I think I've died and gone to lover's heaven."

"What did I tell you?" Ken said to Jan.

"Let the poor brokenhearted boy be," Jan answered.

Everybody laughed but Jerry. He thought he detected a note of sarcasm in Ken's voice, and it bothered him.

As they were nearing town, Ken asked, "So where do we begin tonight?"

"Dick said he would meet us at the Establishment," Patty answered.

"What's that?" Jerry asked.

"It's a place where a lot of kids hang out," Patty replied. "You'll love it."

The Establishment had been started by a community church in Aspen Park. Several years before, the pastor had become concerned for the hundreds of young people who came to Aspen Park to work, and who could find nothing better to do in the evening than to drive back and forth on Main Street, or go to a show. Most of the restaurants and shops were so crowded with tourists that it was impossible for the residents to enjoy themselves. And the kids wanted to get away from tourists for at least one night a week.

So Pastor McConnell had persuaded his board to transform the basement room in the church into an informal coffee house atmosphere. Here young people could come and go at their leisure, and could meet others their own age who worked in the area. Occasionally some transient young people would show up, but since it wasn't highly advertised, most people from outside the area didn't know about it.

The entrance to the Establishment was the basement door of the church. A small neon sign that said "Establishment" was turned on whenever the room was open. Jerry and the group walked through the door, and down the dimly lit basement steps.

"Hey, where are you guys taking me?" Jerry asked.

"Trust us. It's OK," Patty said.

"Trust you? You know what happened the last time I trusted this gang. I was left alone in the woods."

"Just listen, stupid," Ken said, "and you'll know it's just what we said it was."

From behind the next set of doors came sounds of laughter and music. Ken opened the doors and the girls and Jerry stepped into the room. It still looked like a basement with rough rock walls, and an unfinished ceiling, but a glance around the room made you forget the construction. All around — in chairs, on pillows, and standing — were high school and college young people. At one end a fellow in jeans and western-style shirt was strumming a guitar, and several were gathered around him singing a folk song. At the other end of the room an opening in the wall served as a canteen where you could buy coffee, soft drinks, candy, hot dogs, and hamburgers.

"Still think we were trying to double-cross you?" Ken asked.

"This time, you win," Jerry answered. "This looks like a swinging place. Look at the girls. I like it already."

"Before you get too involved," Ken said, "I want you to meet Pastor Mac. He's great."

"You've got to be kidding." Jerry looked surprised. "I want to meet the girls, and you want me to meet a preacher?"

"The girls can come later, you've got plenty of time for that. Besides, this isn't any ordinary preacher."

"He'd better not be."

Ken led Jerry to one side of the room where a group was gathered around an older man. Several recognized Ken and greeted him when he joined the group. The man looked up too, and a big smile came over his face.

63

"Welcome to the Establishment, Ken," he said. "I wondered if you would be back this year."

"Sure," Ken said. "I wouldn't have missed it for anything." Then, turning to Jerry, he said, "Jerry, I want you to meet Pastor Mac. Pastor Mac, I want you to meet a good friend of mine who's working at the ranch this summer, Jerry Fredrickson."

"Hi, Jerry," Pastor Mac said, sticking out his hand.

"Hi," Jerry said, not quite knowing what to say to a preacher.

Jerry and Pastor Mac stood looking at each other for a few moments, sizing each other up. What Jerry saw was a man about 40 with blond hair which was beginning to get thin at the crown. He gave evidence of having been well built in his earlier years, but now he was slightly overweight — especially around the middle. But the thing that captivated Jerry was Pastor Mac's happy face. His eyes seemed to dance every time he spoke.

"I think you'll like it around here, Jerry. We've got food, and lots of friends. Some of the latter variety aren't too bad to look at either. If I read you correctly, you like both."

"Boy, do you read him correctly!" Ken exclaimed.

"You must have been talking," Jerry said.

"Honest, I haven't mentioned you to Pastor Mac. Fact is, this is the first time this year I've seen him."

"Don't worry, Jerry," Pastor Mac said. "I'm not a mind reader, and Ken hasn't been talking. I've just worked with enough guys your age to know what a normal, healthy, American boy is interested in. So enjoy yourself, and stay as long as you like."

Pastor Mac's interest was distracted for a moment, and Jerry looked around the room. Patty had found Dick, and Ken had wandered back toward where Jan was talking to some girls. He saw that there was no one at the canteen counter, so he went over and ordered a cola, then he walked back to a vacant sofa and sat down. He slid down until his head was resting on the back, threw his leg over the arm, and began to drink his cola.

Ordinarily Jerry would have already latched onto some girl and started a conversation, but somehow tonight he just didn't feel like it. After those two weeks with Sue Kelly, it was a good feeling just to be alone. He knew that before the night was over he would probably feel different, but now it was good to just sit and watch.

He sat there for a few minutes, and then Pastor Mac spotted him sitting alone and came over and sat down on the coffee table in front of him. Jerry started to sit up straight, but Pastor

Mac said, "Relax. Don't sit up for me. You've been working hard all week, and you deserve one relaxing night."

"I guess I'm not used to talking to preachers."

"Don't let that preacher handle scare you. Sometimes I wish I didn't have that Rev. before my name. It can cause a false barrier to be set up."

"You don't talk like a preacher."

Pastor Mac laughed. "And what is a preacher supposed to talk like?"

"Oh, he goes around speaking spiritual stuff in a monotone. At least all the preachers I know are that way."

"I'm afraid there are even some preachers who haven't discovered how much fun it is to be a Christian."

"Now you sound like one of the speakers that I heard in Bible Club at school. Only that guy wasn't a preacher, he was just an ordinary guy."

"Maybe the reason I sound like him is that both of us are Christians."

"You mean there are some preachers who aren't?"

"It's possible," Pastor Mac answered. "Being a Christian doesn't depend on what you do for a living. It depends on a personal relationship with Jesus Christ."

"You know, Ken started to tell me about that one time, but we were interrupted, and he never finished. He talked about accepting Christ as Savior."

"That's right. Being a Christian is a matter of allowing Jesus Christ to come into your life."

"You mean it will change my personality?" Jerry asked.

"Not necessarily," Pastor Mac answered. "I think it's more of a change of purpose than of personality. Christ can give you a new purpose for living. However, when some realize this, it changes their personality drastically. For the first time they can really be happy."

"Would becoming a Christian change me?"

"Yes. Even though you seem to have a good, happy outlook on life, and others may not be able to notice much difference, I can guarantee you that Christ would give you strength when you need it, guidance when you ask for it, and a purpose for living. On top of that, He gives eternal life."

"Wow, that's quite a package," Jerry said.

Ken came over to the sofa. "I think we're going to move on."

"Already?" Jerry sounded disappointed. "We just got here."

"I know, but Jan and Patty want to get into some of the stores before they close."

Jerry started to get up.

"Tell you what," Pastor Mac said. "If you really want to stay, I'll take you home later."

"Hey, that sounds great. They don't need me anyway."

"We wouldn't want to leave you here," Jan said, coming up behind Ken.

"That's OK. You four run along. I'll get home some way," Jerry said.

Ken didn't argue.

Jerry spent the remainder of the evening meeting some new kids. He played a couple of games of Ping-Pong with a girl from New Jersey, and beat her both times. When she wouldn't play again, he played some pool with a boy from California. Between games he had more food, and also talked briefly with Pastor Mac. He was beginning to feel much more relaxed in his presence.

Finally, about midnight, most of the kids had left, and Pastor Mac came over to Jerry. "I hate to be a party-pooper, but I have to preach twice tomorrow, so if you're ready, I'll take you home."

"Sure," Jerry said. "It's been a fun evening. I forgot all about the work at the ranch."

Jerry's image of a preacher was even more shaken when they got outside and Pastor Mac led him to a sleek red convertible.

"You mean this is your car?"

"Sure. Can't a preacher enjoy his cars too?"

"Yeah, I suppose so, but it just doesn't fit the picture."

They were quiet as they began the ten-mile

ride to the ranch; both of them were enjoying the peacefulness of the mountains. The sky was dotted with stars and there was a bright moon shining on the snow of Long's Peak.

Jerry broke the silence. "What a night!"

"Kinda makes one glad to be alive. Right?" Pastor Mac replied.

"Yeah. Looks like you could almost reach up and grab one of those stars."

"Sorry, I can't get a star for you," Pastor Mac said, "but I can introduce you to the One who made those stars. Have you thought anymore about our conversation this evening?"

"I sure have, and I'm sold. If that's what being a Christian is all about, I want to be one. What can I do?"

Pastor Mac pulled the car to a stop at one of the scenic turnoff spots along the mountain road, and in the quietness and beauty of a Colorado night, both bowed their heads, and Jerry asked Jesus Christ to come into his life.

7

Heading for Prophet's Peak

Jᴇʀʀʏ ᴏᴘᴇɴᴇᴅ ʜɪꜱ ᴇʏᴇꜱ. He decided it had to be late because the warm sunshine was already streaming through the window and had made a warm spot where it fell on his bed. Nights were generally cool at this altitude, but as soon as the sun came over the mountains and shone through the cloudless Colorado sky, it warmed up quickly.

This was his day off, so he hadn't set the alarm, and he hadn't heard Ken get up. On a normal working day the boys got up about 6:30, but when it was their turn for a day off, they celebrated by sleeping late. No matter what else they had planned for the day, it always began by sleeping in.

Jerry lay for a long time looking up at the ceiling. He had nothing planned for the day, so

71

there was no need to hurry. When he finally decided that he wasn't going back to sleep, he got up. After washing and shaving he put on a checkered western shirt and a clean pair of jeans. Then he headed toward the kitchen to get a late breakfast.

It was a beautiful day. The sky was perfectly clear. There had been a rain the evening before, so the earth still looked fresh and clean. Jerry thought it was the most beautiful day he had ever seen. He stopped for a minute to enjoy the scene and looked up toward the east. There stood Prophet's Peak silhouetted against the morning sky.

"Hey, why not?" he said out loud. He had been talking about climbing the peak ever since he had been at the ranch, but so far there had never been enough time. This would be a perfect day to do it.

He went to the kitchen and got himself a glass of milk and a bowl of cereal. Breakfast had been over for some time, and as yet no one was beginning to prepare lunch, so he was alone in the kitchen. After he had eaten, he went to the refrigerator and found some leftover beef from a barbecue, and made himself a couple of sandwiches. He put them, together with some cookies and an apple, in a sack. Then he went back to the bunkhouse to get his jacket and a canteen. After filling the canteen with water he started following the trail which led in the general direction of Prophet's Peak.

"Look who's mountain climbing today."

Jerry turned around, startled.

"Jan, what are you doing up here?"

"I suppose I could ask the same of you," she said.

"It's my day off, and I just decided to take a walk. OK?"

"It's OK if I can go along," Jan answered.

"Yeah . . . sure, I guess so, but . . ."

". . . but what will Ken say?" she finished it for him.

"Yeah, that's what I was thinking," he said.

"Don't worry about Ken. He'll be working all day. He doesn't know we are here, and he doesn't have time to go looking for us, so let's forget Ken for a little while."

"Well, if that's the way you feel about it."

"That's the way I feel, so come on let's get going. I have to be back to help set tables for dinner this evening. I hope you brought more than one sandwich," she said, looking at the brown bag.

"As a matter of fact, I just happen to have two of almost everything." Jerry laughed.

"Good thinking," Jan said, grabbing his hand and pulling him along the path.

Jerry was too surprised by this turn of events to say much. He had been admiring Jan all summer, and he recognized that Jan had been especially friendly to him, but Ken was his best friend, and one thing he'd never done was come between a friend and his girl.

Jan was as bright and beautiful as the day, and Jerry found himself staring at her whenever he had the chance. Her blonde hair hung loosely about her face and touched her shoulders. He had admired her before, but now, walking by her side, he thought he had never seen her lovelier.

They walked down the path hand in hand when it was wide enough. When it was narrow and steep, Jerry would go ahead, and then reach down and help her up. Each time this happened she gave his hand a little squeeze. Once when he was pulling her up, he lost his balance, and they tumbled to the ground. They lay there for a moment laughing. As Jerry made a move to get up, Jan said, "Let's just rest a bit. OK?"

So they both lay back on the little ledge of rock and looked up through the clearing in the pines to the blue sky above. They were quiet for a little while, then Jan rolled over on her stomach and raised herself up on her elbows so she could look into his face.

"Tell me about yourself, Jerry," she said.

Jerry picked a blade of grass and began to chew on it. "There's not much to tell. I'm just a guy. I take it you noticed that."

"I've noticed."

"Well, let's see . . . I have a father and a mother, one brother and a sister, and we all get along pretty well. I guess that's unusual."

"You can say that again."

"I have a driver's license, but no car. I would love to have a Honda 350, but don't have enough money to buy it. I'll be a senior this fall. I'm an average student, except in swimming — got second in the state last year. Let's see . . . what else? Oh, I like banana cream pie and . . ."

"And girls," Jan said.

"Sure, girls."

"You've always got a harem around you, but don't you ever like just one girl?"

"I like some more than others, if that's what you mean," Jerry answered.

"I wasn't sure, the way you've ignored me."

Jerry sat up. "Look, Jan. I'm as much a wolf as the next guy, and you're pretty hard not to notice, but I haven't chased you for two reasons. First, there's a girl back home who expects me to remain at least somewhat faithful, and second, you're Ken's girl. And Ken and I are too good of friends for me to mess with his girl."

"Ken's girl?" Jan laughed. "The way he acts I sometimes wonder whether he cares anything about me at all."

"Listen, Jan," Jerry was dead serious now, "Ken may not show it, but he likes you very much. He's just a different sort of guy — some-

75

times it's hard for him to show how he feels."

"Aw, come on, Jerry, let's not talk about Ken, let's talk about us," Jan pleaded.

"I tell you there's nothing to talk about," Jerry said as he stood to his feet.

"You're impossible," Jan said.

They started up the path again, only this time in silence, and they weren't holding hands.

After they had gone this way for some time Jan said, "Are you mad?"

"No, a little afraid," he answered.

"Afraid? Of what?"

"Afraid that if I spend much more time with you, I'll forget whose girl you really are."

Jan stopped and took Jerry by the arm. "Then you do like me," she said.

"You're not hard to look at."

"That's the nicest thing you've said to me all summer."

"You know, Jan, I think it would be better for both of us if we went back to the ranch."

"Maybe you're right. But let's at least eat our lunch first."

"Food!" Jerry exclaimed. He was relieved at the change of subject. "Would you believe I have a weakness for food."

"I've noticed," Jan said. "Come on, it's just a little farther to Lone Tree Cabin. We can eat there."

Lone Tree Cabin had been built by the Lost

River Ranch on government land as sort of a halfway resting place for guests who decided to climb Prophet's Peak. It was just a one-room log cabin, with a huge stone fireplace at one end of the room, and a number of low wooden chairs scattered about. Near the fireplace was a large woodbox which was kept filled for the convenience of the guests who became chilly in the high altitude.

When they opened the cabin it looked as if it hadn't been used recently. There were cobwebs on the windows, and the chairs were covered with layers of dust.

"I'll dust off some chairs while you make a fire to get the chill off this room," Jan said.

Jerry took some wood from the box and stacked it neatly in the large grate. He found some matches in a covered tin can on the mantel, and soon he had a warm fire blazing. Jan found a cloth in the broom closet and cleaned off two chairs and then pulled them up to the fireplace so they could put their feet on the stone hearth.

As the room began to get warmer, he took off his jacket, and Jan followed by taking off her sweater. They ate mostly in silence except for some small talk about home and school. When they were through eating, Jan got up and threw the waste papers into the fire, then she went over to the door and pushed it open. She stood in the doorway looking up at Prophet's Peak.

Jerry turned his chair so he could see her.

The sun was shining through the open doorway and reflecting on Jan's soft hair. She was silhouetted against the forested hillside, and there was a smile on her face. Jerry's eyes were riveted on her for a few minutes; then he got up from his chair and went to her side. He leaned against one side of the doorway, and she leaned against the other, and they stood looking into each other's eyes. Finally Jerry could contain himself no longer.

"Did anyone ever tell you you're beautiful?" he asked.

She reached over and touched his cheek with her hand, but did not answer.

He opened his arms, and she dropped into them. He kissed her, and then held her tightly.

They broke away from each other, and Jerry looked off toward the peak. "I think that climbing the peak now would be a big letdown. Let's go back to camp."

They had started to walk away from the cabin when he remembered the door and turned around to shut it.

"Jan?"

"Yes, Jerry?"

"Could we keep this from Ken? I don't know how I would ever explain it to him, not right now anyway."

8

Jerry's Confession

THE SUN WAS SLIPPING behind the continental divide, and its rays were illuminating Prophet's Peak. Supper was over, and Ken and Dick were sitting on the porch of the dining hall. Ken tipped his chair back and placed his boots on the log railing before him. From this position he had the best view of the peak. These few minutes of rest after supper generally coincided with the setting of the sun, and every night the view seemed more spectacular than the last.

Ken's eyes were running aimlessly over the hillside, taking in the beauty of it all, when suddenly he sat up.

"Look over there, Dick," Ken said, pointing in the direction of the peak.

"OK, I'm looking," Dick answered. "What am I supposed to see?"

"Isn't that smoke?" Ken asked, pointing into the distance.

Dick peered in the direction Ken was pointing for a moment, and then he jumped to his feet.

"Not only smoke, I see flames!"

"It looks like it's coming from Lone Tree Cabin," Ken replied.

"We'd better get up there quick," Dick said, "or we might have a forest fire on our hands."

"Where's Jerry?"

"I think he went right to the bunkhouse after supper," Dick answered. "I'll go get him. You get some horses saddled. We can't get there in time by foot."

Ken first ran to Carl's cabin and told him about the fire, then went to the corral and started to saddle a horse. Dick and Jerry came running and saddled two other horses, then they all started out in the direction of the fire. Carl took the jeep and put some fire-fighting equipment in the back and started down the lane to reach the cabin by the old logging road.

The boys reached the cabin first, and the roof on the fireplace end was already blazing. "Let's try to save some of the furniture while we're waiting for Carl," Ken called to the others.

Ken pushed the door open and a blast of hot air and smoke met him. "I'll grab what I can and hand it to you," Ken called to Jerry.

Ken started groping in the darkness. He

found a chair and brought it out to Jerry, and then started back for another. The smoke was so dense that he began to cough, so he came back out and tied a handkerchief across his nose and mouth before going in again. This time he succeeded in finding another chair and went back to the door with it. As he stepped out into the moonlight, his eyes caught something that made him stop short. He looked up to see if anyone was looking. Jerry wasn't back yet, and no one else was close, so he grabbed it and tucked it under his jacket, then carried the chair some distance from the fire. He could feel hot tears begin to run down his cheeks as he returned to the cabin.

By this time Jerry had returned for another load. As the two boys met, Ken stopped for an instant. He looked as if he were about to speak. Jerry looked up, and noticed his wet eyes.

"What's the matter, Ken?"

Ken straightened up. He tried to say something, but nothing came out. Finally he managed, "Nothing. Guess smoke got in my eyes."

"Yeah, it does smart, doesn't it?" Jerry replied.

It was almost midnight when Jerry and Dick returned to the ranch. Carl wanted to stay a little longer at the site of the fire to be sure it was completely out, and Ken volunteered to stay with him. Jerry was glad because he had to have a little time to think. He was mad at himself for not checking the fire before leaving the cabin, and he still wasn't sure how or when he was going to tell Ken about the afternoon.

Instead of going to the bunkhouse, the boys decided to go to the dining hall and get something to eat. They were tired and hungry after their ordeal. As they stepped on the porch, a figure got up from one of the chairs. It was too dark to recognize who it was until a voice said, "Jerry?"

"Jan, what are you doing up?" Jerry asked.

"Can I talk to you?" Jan's voice sounded serious.

"Sure, but. . ."

"I know when I'm not wanted." Dick laughed. "I'll see you in the morning, Jerry." With that Dick disappeared into the dining hall.

Jerry pulled up a chair beside Jan.

"Did we do it?" she said in a low voice.

"I'm afraid so," Jerry answered.

"Have you told Daddy?"

"No, I'll tell him in the morning."

"Why do you have to?"

" 'Cause. We did it, and he should know. I wouldn't want him blaming one of the guests."

"But if he finds out he will be furious." Jan sounded as if she were going to cry.

"Think how furious he will be if we don't tell him, and he finds out some other way."

"But if he doesn't find out?"

"But . . . that's just not right."

"Why?" she insisted.

"Well, I haven't been a Christian very long, but I've had some long talks with Pastor Mac since that first time we met, and I'm learning how having Christ in your life changes you. I know Christ expects me to be honest. I feel rotten about this whole thing, and I hate to tell your dad as much as you do. He might even fire me, but I'd feel a lot worse if I didn't tell."

"But I don't see anything dishonest about not telling him. You're not telling him a lie."

"But if I deliberately lead him into thinking something that isn't true, isn't that a lie?"

"If you're going to be so honest about the fire, then why didn't you tell Ken about us?" she asked.

Jerry was silent. "Somehow that doesn't seem the same," he finally said.

"Why isn't it?" Jan asked. "By not telling him you're leading him into thinking that he and I have a big thing between us."

This time Jerry didn't have an answer. He got to his feet, and stood for a moment looking out into the darkness. Then he slowly turned and began walking down the steps.

"Jerry," Jan called.

But he didn't answer. He walked slowly back to the bunkhouse and found his way to his bed without turning on the lights. He was too tired, and too mixed up to think straight. He just pulled off his boots and lay back on the bed without undressing.

Jerry woke up with a start. The warm sun was shining down on him. He looked down at his clothes, and it all came back to him like a nightmare. He turned to the bunk beside him, but Ken wasn't there, and it was obvious that he hadn't been there all night.

He got up and went into the bathroom. He was surprised by what he saw in the mirror. There was a dirty smudge across one cheek, and his hair was hanging in a tangled mess. Jerry tried to clean his face, but the events of the night kept coming back to him, and it was hard to concentrate. He was vaguely aware that he was hungry.

After changing into some clean clothes, and pulling on a clean pair of boots, he stepped out into the bright morning light. He hadn't thought of looking at the clock, and had no idea of what time it was, but the activities around the ranch told him that it had to be mid-morning.

Why hadn't someone awakened him? Where was Ken? His mind kept racing back and forth from question to question. He went to the dining hall, but it was empty. He went to the kitchen and got himself some cereal and milk and sat down at the table in the crew's kitchen. He was conscious of a splitting headache, and went to the cupboard and got a couple of aspirins.

He was still eating his cereal when the door opened and Carl came into the kitchen.

"Morning, Jerry," he said.

"Where is everyone? Why didn't someone wake me up?"

"We all had a pretty rough night," Carl answered. "So I didn't wake anyone up. I thought the guests would understand for once."

"But where is Ken?" Jerry asked as he picked up his dishes and carried them over to the sink. "He wasn't in all night."

"I know," Carl said. "He was with me most of the night."

"But where is he now?"

Carl acted as if he didn't hear the question. "When you finish eating would you come down to the office?"

"Sure, Carl. I'll be right down."

Carl left, and Jerry sat down to think. So this was it. Carl was going to ask him about the fire. What was he going to tell him?

Jerry got up and began to walk slowly down to the office. It suddenly seemed that he was much older than yesterday. He was tired, and ashamed, and his head was still pounding. How would Carl react? Maybe he shouldn't have come to the ranch. Right now he wished he'd never met Ken, or Jan, or heard of Lost River Ranch.

Carl was sitting behind his desk when Jerry

came in. He turned his chair and motioned for him to sit down.

"Tell me, Jerry," he began. "What do you know about the fire yesterday?"

This was the question Jerry had been dreading. He hung his head for a minute, and found himself praying, "Lord, please help me."

"I ..." He cleared his throat, and began again. "I started to walk up to Prophet's Peak yesterday."

"Were you alone?" Carl asked.

Jerry looked into Carl's eyes, and knew that he had to tell the truth. "No, sir."

"And who was with you?"

"I met Jan along the way."

"And it was the two of you who were in the cabin and built the fire?"

"Yes. We forgot to put it out. Can you forgive me?"

"Yes, Jerry. I forgive you. And I'm glad you told me the truth. You see, Ken gave these to me. He found them in the cabin." Carl reached behind his desk and pulled out a sweater and a jacket.

Jerry's lips tightened. It was his coat and Jan's sweater. They had left them in the cabin.

He reached out and took them. "Thanks, Carl."

"Like I say," Carl continued, "I forgive you. It was a careless thing to do, but it was an accident. However, I'm not sure it's going to be so easy for Ken to forgive you. I guess he likes Jan a lot, and he's pretty upset about the whole thing."

"We . . . I didn't think he would find out so soon. I really meant to tell him. Do you know where he is?"

"No, but I think you'd better try to find him and get this thing straightened out. I'd hate to see it break up your friendship."

Jerry left the office and took the sweater and jacket to the bunkhouse. He checked to see if any of the camp vehicles were gone, and when none was missing, he decided that Ken had to be somewhere in the area. He searched the horse barn, the pavilion, and even walked around the cabins, but saw no trace of Ken. The only place left for him to look was the mountains, so he started up one of the trails.

After walking for about half an hour, Jerry came to the little clearing where they had stopped that first night when they were initiating him. From this clearing one could see the entire valley. There, sitting on the rocky ledge, was Ken. His knees were drawn up under his chin, and he was staring out at the valley below.

Ken didn't move as Jerry approached, nor did he act as if he had heard anyone. Jerry sat down beside him. Neither looked at the other, and neither spoke.

It was Jerry who broke the silence. "What are you doing here?" he said.

"I could ask you the same thing," Ken answered.

"I have to talk to you."

"So."

Jerry looked out over the valley, then he began, "A lot of things have happened since we first stood here."

Ken was silent.

"Ken," he said, looking directly at him, "I'm sorry about yesterday. Would you believe me if I said I didn't plan it that way?"

"Just what did happen yesterday?"

"You've got to believe me," Jerry pleaded. "I didn't plan it. It just happened."

"But I'm asking you, what happened?"

"Nothing. Really. I started out on a hike, and before I knew it, Jan was tagging along. We stopped at the cabin to eat, and I built a fire because it was cold in there."

"Is that all?"

"You know my weakness for girls. I tried to remind myself that she was your girl, but I couldn't resist her. So I kissed her. Just once, that's all. Like I said, I'm sorry."

"Some friend you turn out to be. The minute my back is turned you're running off into the mountains with the one person I care about."

"It wasn't like that at all!" Jerry answered,

half shouting. "But I can see you're going to believe what you want. And besides, if you care so much about Jan, you sure have a funny way of showing it."

"Just because I'm not one of the world's great lovers like yourself," was Ken's reply, but Jerry was already on his way back down the mountain.

9

Lost in the Woods

ONCE EACH WEEK the ranch provided an overnight for guests who wanted to camp out. The crew would prepare the site and set up the tents. Then following the evening meal the guests would be taken to the campsite.

The road to the site was a narrow, winding, logging trail which only a jeep with four-wheel drive could successfully maneuver. The guests were generally taken by bus to a pasture about two miles from the site, and then they would walk the rest of the way.

Ken and Dick had been working throughout the afternoon setting up camp. Carl had decided to use a different spot for this overnight, so besides setting up the two large tents, the boys built a crude stone fireplace and arranged some logs around it for the sing-along.

"Looks like we're ready for the mob," Ken said, surveying the site. "Let's go back to camp and get some grub."

The boys got into the jeep and drove back over the rocky path to the main trail, then to the dirt road that eventually wound its way down to the blacktop leading back to the ranch.

Following dinner, the guests who were to go on the overnight gathered on the porch of the dining hall with their sleeping bags and equipment. Dick brought the bus around, and Jerry and Ken were there to help the guests load.

Since the episode with the fire, they both had been polite, but distant with each other. They knew that if they wanted to keep their jobs, they had to at least be able to work together.

They started out with the jeep, which contained the food for the evening snack and breakfast, and Dick followed, driving the bus. The plan was for Ken and Jerry to go ahead to the site and start the fire, while Dick parked the bus and led the guests to the spot.

It was just beginning to get dusk when they arrived at the campsite. It was on the eastern slope of the mountains, and darkness came rapidly once the sun set behind the peaks.

"Hope Dick remembered to bring some flashlights," Jerry said as he started to unload.

"I hope he remembers how to find this new spot."

When the jeep was unloaded, and the firewood was arranged, ready to be lit, Ken and Jerry sat down on one of the logs.

"Shouldn't they be here by now?" Jerry asked.

"Seems so. Can you hear anything?"

Both boys were quiet for a minute. In the distance they could hear some talking and laughing.

"I hear them," Jerry said, "but they should be closer than that."

"And the sounds seem to be coming from the north. If that's true, they missed the turnoff, and are headed straight up Turkey Canyon."

"Come on, we'd better try to catch them."

"We don't have much time to lose," Ken said, looking toward the last rays of the setting sun.

Ken and Jerry got into the jeep and retraced their tracks back to the fork in the road. There they stopped and examined the ground.

"Sure enough," Ken said, pointing to the ground, "there are their footprints, and they turned the wrong way."

They got back into the jeep and headed in the direction the guests had taken, but after a few yards the road became impassable, even for the jeep. This time they stopped the jeep and shut off the motor. They strained their ears, but only once did they think they heard voices.

"I can't believe it," Ken exclaimed. "How could they get lost so fast?"

Ken stood up in the seat of the jeep and shouted, but all they could hear was the returning echo of his voice. Jerry blew the horn, but there was no answer, no response. It seemed that the night was becoming more and more silent all the time.

"OK, mountaineer," Jerry said, "now what do we do?"

"I may have been here before, but I was never so stupid as to lose a whole busload of guests," Ken answered. "I guess we just take our flashlights and start looking."

"Oh, fine. A flashlight in 10,000 acres of mountains. What good will that do?"

"You got a better idea?"

"First, I think we should go back to camp and get a good fire going. Maybe they can see it and get a sense of direction," Jerry answered.

"I wish I had thought of that," Ken said. "Let's go."

They were able to back the jeep down the trail to the fork, and then drive back to the site. This time they piled extra logs on the fire and started them burning. By now the last rays of the sun were gone, and since there was no moon, the only light came from the flames.

After waiting for about half an hour without any sound of Dick and the guests, the boys began to get restless. Jerry put some more wood on the fire, and Ken began pacing back and forth.

"I still think we should be doing something," Ken said.

"Yeah, it does seem a little silly to just sit here and wait."

"Tell you what we'll do. You stay here and keep the fire going, and I'll try to follow the tracks up that road. If you keep the fire going, I can't get lost."

"You'd better not," Jerry said. "If they come back another way we don't want to have to go out looking for you."

So Ken took the flashlight he had found in the jeep and started out on foot while Jerry sat down on a log before the fire.

It was getting chilly, so he buttoned up his jacket. In the distance he could hear an occasional car as it traveled along the blacktop road on the other side of the valley. The only other sounds came from a mountain stream about 100 feet from the campsite.

Sitting alone in the stillness gave Jerry a funny sensation. He had spent all his life in the city, and its sounds had become such a part of him that the silence here was deafening. He tried to think about home, but it seemed so far away both in miles and in time. He thought about his parents, his brother . . . and Ann. He wondered what she was doing and if she was thinking about him.

Suddenly a twig cracked behind him. He

bolted up on his feet and peered into the darkness. Without taking his eyes off the direction the sound came from, he felt his way to where he had left the flashlight. He slowly brought it up, and turned it on. He aimed it in the direction of the noise, but there was nothing but empty darkness.

"This silence must be getting to me," he muttered to himself. "Must have been just the fire cracking."

But he had only been sitting for a few minutes when he heard the noise again. This time it came from the opposite side of the jeep. First there was the cracking of twigs, and then he could hear some paper rattling.

Picking up the flashlight again, he remained in a crouched position and made his way cerefully and silently to the jeep. He pulled himself up along one side, and turned on the flashlight. With the flash, a head turned, and two eyes shone out of the darkness. After one brief look, the animal turned and began to run. Jerry could see in his light the black fur of a mountain bear. In its haste to leave, the bear had knocked over a box of groceries beside the jeep.

This was the first time since he'd been at Lost River Ranch that he'd seen a bear. He had heard plenty of bear stories, and had seen where they had been in the garbage behind the kitchen, but he had never actually seen one.

Jerry was surprised at his reaction. He really wasn't as afraid as he thought he might be. He picked up the box of groceries, flashed his light into the woods a couple of times, put some more logs on the fire, and sat down.

He had only been sitting a little while when he again heard sounds in the woods. This time, however, they were voices. He jumped to his feet and turned on his light. This time, instead of a bear, he recognized Dick's red plaid shirt.

"Dick, is that you?" he called.

"Right," Dick called back. "At last!"

"Is Ken with you?"

"Ken?" Dick's voice sounded puzzled. "No, we haven't seen anything of him."

By this time Dick and the 30 guests were beginning to come into the light of the campfire.

"But, he left here an hour ago looking for you."

"Oh, boy! That's all we need — somebody else lost!"

"How about the group?" Jerry asked. "Are they all OK?"

"Several got pretty wet when we crossed a stream," Dick answered. "Otherwise I think they're OK. Sure glad you kept a fire going. We saw the flame, and just followed it here."

"So what do we do about Ken?" Jerry asked.

"Beats me. Maybe he'll find his way back just like we did."

"But you weren't alone."

97

"That's right, but if we go looking for him we'll need some help."

Jerry stepped up on a log so everyone could see him. "We're all terribly sorry that things turned out this way. You're welcome to discuss it with Carl tomorrow, but right now we have a decision to make. We still have a man lost. Ken went looking for you, and hasn't returned. It's up to you. Do you want Dick to take you back to the ranch now so that you can dry out, or should we look for Ken first?"

Everyone was quiet for a moment, and then one lady said, "Well, I'm wet, but I should be able to dry out by the fire. I say we stay."

"That's right," another said. "After all, he was out looking for us."

"Of course, if he had gone with us in the first place we might never have gotten ourselves lost," a woman from Texas drawled.

One of the men stepped into the light and said, "We all signed up for a night in the mountains. Well, we're here, so let's make the most of it."

A chorus of "right" met his statement.

"If that's the way you feel," Jerry said, "we need about four or five men who will volunteer to go with us. That way we can spread out, and by staying within shouting distance of one another, we can cover quite an area. I know which way he started, so we should be able to cover the general area. Who will go with me?"

Within a few minutes he had organized a party of men with flashlights. They planned a system of calls whereby they could check with each other periodically. Dick decided to stay at camp and supervise the preparation of some food to have ready when they returned.

After almost an hour of walking the men decided, through calls, to assemble and decide what to do next. They met on top of a little knoll and sat down. The moon was coming up, and in a little while the search would be easier with the light of a full moon.

"Did anyone see any clues?" Jerry asked.

They all answered, "No."

It was quiet for a minute, then Jerry said, "What was that?"

"What was what?" one of the men said.

"I thought I heard a voice," Jerry answered in a whisper.

"It might have been an animal. There are lots of them out here."

Jerry smiled to himself as he thought of the bear back at camp. "Yeah, there are a few," he said. "But, I'm sure I heard a human voice."

They were quiet again, then Jerry called, "Ken, Ken, is that you?"

And off in the distance there was a definite response, but they couldn't be certain if it was another voice, or just the echo of Jerry's voice.

They got up. A couple of the men cupped

their ears, and once more Jerry called, "Ken! Ken!"

"I'm down here," came a distant reply.

"It's him all right!" Jerry exclaimed. "We'll be right there!"

"Come on," he said to the men. "He must be this way."

They went a few yards, and Jerry called again. This time the answer was more distinct, so they knew they were going in the right direction. When they got close enough so they could hear better, Jerry called, "Can you come to us?"

"Nope, you'll have to get me," Ken replied.

"Are you hurt?"

"Just a busted ankle," came the reply.

"Where are you?"

"I'm down here by the stream. Be careful so you don't come down the way I did."

The men began to pick their way more carefully. Then by the light of the moon they saw the deep cut made by the mountain stream.

"Are we getting close?" Jerry called.

"Sounds as if you're right above me," Ken replied.

"How do we get down there?"

"Carefully," Ken answered.

"Quit clowning. You've kept us up half the night already."

"Who's with you?"

"Some of your lost guests."

The men searched until they found a way down to the edge of the stream. It was a 25-foot drop to the water, but they were able to find a place where the bank wasn't too steep to descend.

When they got to Ken, he said to Jerry, "Boy, am I glad to see you. Never thought I'd see the day when you had to come looking for me in the woods."

"You had to find me once." Jerry laughed.

They hadn't come prepared for a broken bone, but by using a couple of straight sticks, and two large handkerchiefs, they rigged up something that could keep the ankle rather rigid while they half carried Ken back to camp.

It was past three in the morning when they all sat down around the fire. Some had dozed off, but most of the guests were still sitting around, drinking coffee, and just waiting.

Ken told how that after he realized he couldn't find anyone, he had tried to go back to camp, but had gotten lost. He had heard water, and remembered that one way out of the mountains was to follow a stream.

When he came to the stream he found that it was in a ravine with steep sides. So he had started to edge his way along the ledge above, and had gone several yards when he felt the ground give way beneath him. He landed on his feet in the water below, and the impact was enough to snap a bone in his ankle.

101

After Ken had told his story to the group, he said, "Well, that's all there's to it. The question is, what do we do now?"

Jerry found some aspirins in the first-aid kit in the jeep and gave them to Ken. "I think we had all better go back to the ranch," he said. "We've got to get you to the hospital, and I think the night is pretty well shot for the rest of us."

They all agreed with Jerry.

So they put out the fire, made a bed in the back of the jeep with some sleeping bags, and with Jerry driving the jeep and Dick the bus, they all went back to the ranch.

The next morning most of the guests decided to sleep in. Ken was resting in the Aspen Park Hospital with a cast on his foot, and Jerry, after getting back from town about sunup, had dropped on his bed without taking off his clothes and had fallen asleep.

10

Unexpected News

KEN'S INJURY added to the work load of the rest of the staff. He spent the weekend in the hospital, but by Monday he was back at the ranch walking on crutches. His one foot was in a cast which reached almost to his knee. The doctor said it was a clean break, and with no complications he should have the cast off in about four weeks.

Ken had decided that he was through working for the summer, but after talking to Carl about it, he decided to stay on. Carl agreed to let Ken take more of the office work, and since it was his left leg that was in a cast, it was possible for him to drive Carl's car with an automatic transmission. He could make some of the daily trips into town for Carl.

Jerry continued to be lifeguard in the afternoons, but in the mornings he took over some of Ken's regular duties. Carl hired one neighbor girl to come in at mealtime to relieve Jan so she could spend more time cleaning cabins, which had also been one of Ken's chores. All of this had been decided at a staff meeting while Ken was in the hospital. Everyone had agreed to take on a little more work so Ken could stay on for the remainder of the summer.

One afternoon while Ken was resting on his bed, the bunkhouse door was kicked open and Jerry called, "Ken, Ken!"

"I'm here. Stop your yelling. Can't you see I'm sleeping?" Ken replied.

"You're not now," Jerry said as he dropped on the bed across from Ken and held up a letter. "Guess what's in this."

"Who knows? Probably a letter from the President," Ken said dryly.

"No such luck. Ken, she's coming!"

"She? Who's coming?" Ken propped himself up on his elbow to get a better look at Jerry.

"Ann's coming! Ann's coming for a whole week."

"Oh, boy!" Ken said, dropping his head back on the pillow. "That's all we need — another female for you to worry about."

"Ken, you've got to help me. If she finds out I've been dating Jan this summer, I'm dead.

I'm not even sure how I feel about Ann right now. A few weeks and a few hundred miles can make a lot of difference, you know."

"As I see it, it's your problem," Ken answered. "You didn't have to promise Ann you'd be true to her, and you didn't have to fall for every girl you met here."

"I didn't."

"So, Lover Boy, when does trouble arrive?"

Jerry removed the letter from the envelope. "She says here that she and her parents have reserved a cabin for the week of August 11-18. Let's see . . . ," he pulled his wallet from his hip pocket, and took out a calendar. "Let's see . . . that's just two weeks from next Sunday."

"When I'm not with the one I love, I love the one I'm with," Ken started to sing.

"Aw, come off it," Jerry said. "You're jealous."

"Me, jealous? I'm too old and too wise."

"I don't believe you," Jerry said.

"Look, kid. We've been through this before. I'm happy for you. But just remember, you got yourself into this, and old Ken is not about to help you out when Ann gets here."

"Thanks, pal. I think I'll just go and kill myself," Jerry said, stuffing the letter in his pocket. "I'll remember this when you get yourself in a jam."

"Even if I agreed to help, what could I do?" Ken said, lifting his leg off the bed and sitting up.

Jerry looked slightly relieved. "For one week you could make it look as if you were going with Jan again. Maybe you could even take her someplace so that she wouldn't be hanging around."

"I thought you liked her hanging around."

"I do, but not with another girl looking on."

"Let me get this straight. You took my girl from me, and now you want me to knock myself out entertaining her so that when Ann leaves you can have her back again?"

"OK! So it sounds rotten."

"Do you really think I don't care . . . that I'm neutral in all of this?"

"Then you *are* jealous?" Jerry said.

"Not exactly jealous. I know when I'm licked, but if I thought for one minute that you were just fooling around and didn't really care, I'd flatten you."

"Then you do still like Jan."

"Sure I do, and you know it. You knew it when you started going with her. Look, Jerry, if I start chasing Jan again, it won't be just to keep her out of the way while Ann is here. I've learned a few things watching you this summer."

"Can I think that one over?"

"Sure, but understand this. I'll do my best to keep Jan away from you and Ann, but I'll also do my best to get her away from you. That should be fair enough."

That night after the sing-along and the skits

were over, and most of the guests had gone to their cabins, Jerry sat down on the porch of the dining hall to think. He leaned back in the big wooden rocker and put his feet up on the porch railing. A bright moon was out, and he could see the outline of Prophet's Peak silhouetted against the night sky.

"Funny," he thought to himself. "Funny how peaceful all nature seems to be. It's so orderly, so quiet, and here on earth everything gets so mixed up." He dropped his head in his hands and prayed, "Lord . . . Lord of all nature, give me some of Your peace and strength. Help me to make some sense out of my life."

"Why, Jerry, I thought you had gone to bed." It was Jan.

"It's too beautiful a night," Jerry replied, lifting his head.

"I didn't know you were that big on nature — at least not when you're alone," Jan said, pulling up a chair beside him.

"I just feel like it tonight."

"You want me to leave you alone?"

"Naw, stick around. I've got something to tell you anyway."

"Sounds interesting. What's on your mind?" Jan reached over and laid her hand softly on his arm.

Jerry looked at Jan. In the light of the moon he could see her face framed by the arched back of the rocker. Her hair hung loosely around her face and touched her shoulders.

"Let's go for a walk," he said.

"I thought you wanted to tell me something."

"It can wait. Right now let's enjoy this moon. We can't let all that moon go to waste."

They walked along hand in hand. First they went across the grounds, and then down the lane. When they got to the entrance gate, Jan leaned against the post, and Jerry stood facing her. He took her other hand and they stood there face to face for a few minutes. It was Jan who broke the silence.

"And now what is it you wanted to tell me?"

"Oh, that . . ." Jerry stammered. "I . . . I just wanted to tell you that you're beautiful."

"Wow, that was quite a production for that news, but thanks just the same."

They both laughed. Jerry seemed relieved, and they looked at their watches and decided it was time to go to bed.

When Jerry came into the bunkhouse he was whistling. Ken was already in bed, but he was lying there with his eyes wide open.

"Sounds like you had a good time," Ken said.

Instead of undressing, Jerry sat on the edge of his bed so he could face Ken. "I tried. I tried . . . really tried to tell her about Ann, but I'm sorry, Ken, I just couldn't do it."

"So I take it our little deal is off?"

"I don't know what I'm going to do, but I just can't risk losing Jan. I'm sorry ol' man."

Ken blinked his eyes, and turned his face toward the wall.

There was complete silence. Then Ken said, "Shut off the lights, so I can get some sleep."

Jerry undressed, turned off the lights, and crawled into bed, but he didn't go to sleep for a long time.

11

Ann's Arrival

THE FOLLOWING TWO WEEKS were filled with work. Jerry and Ken spoke to each other, but neither of them mentioned Ann's coming.

Ken's leg was healing to the satisfaction of the doctor, so the cast was removed just the day before Ann and her parents arrived at Lost River Ranch.

"I suppose you'll be going back to the pool full time next week?" Ken said to Jerry one night.

"Haven't talked to Carl, but I suppose so. That means that Dick can take back his lawn mowing, and you can take your stagecoach from Dick."

Another feature of the ranch was a stagecoach ride. Each afternoon Ken would hitch two horses to a replica of a 19th-century stagecoach, and give rides to the guests. The route for those rides was over a trail through the woods that had actually been a stagecoach route in about 1860. Following Ken's injury, Dick had taken over the rides temporarily.

"All day at the pool should give you more time with the women again," Ken said sarcastically.

"Aw, quit needling me," Jerry snapped. "You know that I've been leaving the guests alone."

"I've noticed. Of course, you've been so busy with the staff that you really haven't had much time left for the guests."

This time Jerry ignored Ken's remark, and both went to sleep without saying anything more.

Ann and her parents arrived on the scheduled day. As usual, Jerry and the other members of the staff were at the office to help the new guests get settled. When the Hamiltons arrived, Jerry went out to the car to greet them, and since they also knew Ken, he followed Jerry to the car.

"Hi, Jerry," Ann called from out of the car window.

"Hi, beautiful," Jerry said, flashing his usual broad smile.

Ann got out of the car. "Let me look at you," she said, walking around him.

"So, what's wrong with me?" he asked.

"I'm just making sure that you're all right. And let's see those arms. . . ." She felt both arms. "I guess they're OK too. From the number of letters you wrote, I wasn't sure."

"He's been pretty busy," Ken volunteered.

Jerry glanced at Ken. It was evident that Ken had meant it as a cutting remark.

"Yeah, I guess I have been pretty busy," Jerry said.

"Aren't you even going to say hello to us?" Ann's father called.

"Oh, sorry," Jerry said. "Welcome to Lost River Ranch. And how are you, Mrs. Hamilton?"

"Just fine. Your mother and father both sent their greetings. They were complaining about not having heard from you."

Ken came over to the car and greeted the Hamiltons. After the greetings were over, Jerry said, "If you'll just follow me, I'll show you to your cabin."

"While he's doing that, how about letting me show you around the ranch, Ann?" Ken said.

Ann looked toward Jerry, but he had already started to walk away. "Great, Ken," she said. "You can tell me if Jerry's been good."

Jerry overheard the remark and turned around. "That is one conversation I would like to hear," he exclaimed.

It was after supper that evening before Ann had a chance to talk to Jerry alone. The crew had eaten in the staff kitchen as usual, and Ann had eaten with her parents in the dining hall. After supper Jerry sat down on the porch as usual.

"Well, stranger, aren't you going to ask me to join you?" Ann said, coming out of the dining hall.

"Be my guest," Jerry said, pulling a chair over near his.

"Has it been a good summer for you?" Ann began, after a somewhat awkward silence.

"I've learned a lot, if that's what you mean," Jerry answered.

"You've changed too."

"How do you mean that?" he asked.

"The Jerry I remember was a happy-go-lucky kid who didn't seem to care about anything."

"And now?"

"Now. Well, now you seem so businesslike — so grown up."

"I suppose for one thing I've had more time to think out here. It's amazing what a walk up there in those mountains can do for a person." He pointed in the direction of Prophet's Peak.

He continued. "I've learned a lot about myself, and a lot more about God this summer. You just seem to be closer to God out here under the stars, and moonlight."

"Did I hear something about moonlight?" Jerry hadn't heard Jan come up behind them.

"You weren't supposed to be listening," Jerry said, laughing. "Jan, I want you to meet a friend of mine from back home. Jan, this is Ann Hamilton. Ann, this is Jan Johnson."

114

"Glad to meet you, Ann," Jan said, pulling up another chair on the opposite side of Jerry.

"Didn't I see you helping serve tonight?" Ann said.

"That's right. This is my home. My dad is the manager here, so we live here the year around."

"Imagine living in a place like this! It must be paradise," Ann exclaimed.

"It's nice, but it's much more fun in the summer when there are so many others around . . . especially this summer with Jerry here."

Jerry could feel his face beginning to flush.

"You can imagine what it's been like around home without him all summer," Ann said.

There was a silence, and it was obvious to Jerry that the girls were reading each other loud and clear, and he was caught in the middle.

Ken saved the day for him by coming out of the dining hall just then and jumping up on the rail in front of Ann. "It's sure good to see someone from back home," he said to her.

"You make it sound as if we haven't treated you very well," Jan said.

"It's not that, but it hasn't been exactly the best summer for me, you know. Being laid up with that busted ankle for four weeks isn't my idea of fun. If I hadn't felt responsible for Jerry, I probably would have gone home."

"You make yourself sound like a big brother," Jerry said.

"Somebody needs to play big brother to you," Ken answered. He was smiling, but Jerry felt the sting of his words.

"I'm beginning to think that I need to hear more," Ann said.

"Maybe we had better go for a walk so I can tell you the gruesome details," Ken said.

"Up there?" Ann said, pointing to the mountains.

"Not all the way, my ankle is still weak, you know."

"Let's go," Ann replied. "Jerry told me that a walk in the mountains was good for one's soul."

Jerry cringed and looked at Jan. He half expected to hear some cutting remark from her, but all she said was, "I've got to get ready for the skit that Patty and I are giving to the guests tonight. Think I'd better go."

So Jerry found himself alone once again — and really thinking this time.

When Ken came to the bunkhouse that night he didn't mention his walk, or Ann. With the exception of a couple of casual remarks, he was silent. Jerry started to ask him about his talk with Ann several times, but each time he decided against it.

During the next few days Ann was still friendly to Jerry, but she made no more attempts to talk to him alone. Ken, on the other hand, began spending as much time with her as he could. He showed up wherever Ann was. If she went riding, he just happened to be the guide for that trip. If he drove the guests in the stagecoach, Ann always decided to go for a stage ride that day. By Thursday night Jerry could stand the silence no longer. When they were both in bed that night, Jerry said, "OK, Ken, what gives with you and Ann?"

"I don't see why you should care," Ken answered.

"Maybe I don't, but I've never seen you go so overboard with a girl before. What's your game? Are you trying to teach little Jerry a lesson?"

Ken sat up on the edge of the bed and stared across the darkened room. "Look, you've got what you want, and you seem to be enjoying it. Ann's a nice girl and I enjoy being with her. Is that a crime?"

"OK," Jerry said hesitatingly, "but it just isn't like you. Jan said you never treated her like that."

"Maybe I didn't have to. Nobody else was chasing her."

"You brought me out here, you know."

"There are times when I'm sorry I did."

Jerry didn't answer, and after a period of silence, Ken lay back down, and neither said anything more that night.

12

A Runaway Stagecoach

THE FOLLOWING AFTERNOON Ken hitched up
the horses to the stagecoach as usual. Six people
had signed up for the ride, including Ann. Ken
had been reluctant to do it before, but this time
he invited her to sit in the driver's seat with him.

It was a happy, laughing group that started
down the road. The route took them the two
miles to the main road, then back via a road
which had been constructed especially to con-
nect with the old stagecoach road. That trail
led directly back to the ranch. The total trip
was about five miles, and Ken usually made two
trips each afternoon.

It was a beautiful day. A bright blue Colorado
sky was overhead, and around them were the
light green aspen. In the distance they could
see the dark green pine trees. Ann sat close to

Ken. As they rode along they talked about school, and kids they both knew. The horses knew the road because they had been this way so many times before, so Ken could devote all of his attention to Ann.

As they approached a section of the road where the grade became steeper, Ken automatically leaned over and pulled the lever by the side of his seat which applied the brakes to the stage. It was necessary to do this to keep the coach from overtaking the horses. As he pulled the lever he realized to his horror that it was no longer connected to the brake cable. It hung loose in his hands.

"Oh, boy!" Ken exclaimed. "Are we in trouble!"

"What happened?" Ann asked.

"We've lost our brakes," Ken answered. "Hang onto me. We may have trouble stopping this thing."

The stage started to roll free, and the horses began to feel the push of the tongue on their collars. To compensate for this they began to speed up their pace, but that only made the stage go faster. Ken was hanging onto the reins and calling, "Whoa, whoa," at the top of his voice, but the horses simply could not stop.

When Ken saw that he couldn't get the horses stopped, he called back to the people in the coach, "Everyone hang onto the strap beside you; we may have to crash."

Some of the passengers began to scream, and Ann hung onto Ken with both arms. Ken dropped one rein, and began to pull as hard as he could on the other to force the horses to run toward the steep bank on the one side of the road. As he pulled, the horses finally began to edge that way. He could hear the people screaming in the coach, and Ann had buried her face in his jacket so she couldn't see what was ahead. When one wheel hit the edge of the road, it jerked the stagecoach in that direction, but just then they rounded a small curve, and Ken saw a tree directly in their path.

"We're going to hit!" Ken screamed. "Hang on tight!"

There was a crash, and the sound of splintering wood. The hitch broke with the impact, and the horses broke away. As the coach hit, Ken and Ann were thrown off their seats and onto the ground.

Ken momentarily blacked out, but when he came to he could hear someone crying, and the horses galloping off into the distance. His first thought was of his leg since he had only had the cast off for a few days. He tried to stand, and found that it didn't hurt. Then he thought about the guests. The tree had hit the front right corner of the coach, and smashed that corner. He jerked open the door and called.

"Anybody hurt?"

"I don't think so," a lady said, "but this little boy got a pretty nasty bump on his head." They all began to scramble out of the coach. Then Ken remembered Ann.

"Ann. Ann," he called. "Where are you?"

"Look! Over there!" A guest pointed to a form lying face down some distance from the coach.

Ken ran over to Ann. He turned her over on her back. Blood was beginning to spill from a cut on her temple.

"Oh, Ann," he said, pulling out a handkerchief and wiping some of the blood from her face.

"Let me have a look," one of the ladies said. "I'm a nurse."

Someone got a water canteen he had brought along, and the nurse used Ken's handkerchief to put some cool water on Ann's forehead. She stirred, and a sigh of relief went through the group. Even the boy who had been crying forgot his hurt, and stood in awe at the sight of the blood.

"If only I hadn't let her ride with me," Ken was saying out loud. "Carl told us never to let a guest ride with us in the driver's seat. I'd better go get some help."

Ken started to run, but a few strides reminded him that his ankle wasn't completely healed. So he began to walk as fast as he could. He hadn't gone very far, however, when he heard the jeep coming. He looked up to see Dick racing up the trail in a cloud of dust. At the sight of Ken, he slid the jeep to a halt.

"What happened?" he asked in an excited voice.

"The brakes gave out. And Ann's hurt."

"The horses came home, and the wagon tongue was still between them, so I knew something happened. How about the other people?"

"They're OK, but we've got to get help for Ann; she's still unconscious."

Ken jumped in and they drove up to the scene of the accident. Dick took one look at Ann, and then talked to the nurse.

"I think it's just a bad bump on the head," the nurse said. "She should come out of it before long, but we had better not take any chances. I'll stay here with her while you go call an ambulance."

So Dick loaded up the guests in the jeep, and started back down the road. Ken decided to stay with Ann and the nurse. He wanted to stay, and besides there wasn't room for him in the jeep.

As they were waiting, Ken paced back and forth between Ann and the coach. Once he walked over and leaned against the wheel. As he looked down at the ground, his eye caught the end of the broken cable. He began to examine it, and then picked up the broken ends. He stared in disbelief. There was no mistake about it — someone had cut through the cable.

123

Jerry was just closing up the pool for the afternoon when Dick got back. He wondered why Dick was driving so fast. He had missed seeing the horses come back, and Dick had taken off without mentioning it to anyone.

Dick brought the jeep to a sliding stop in front of the office building. As he jumped out, he yelled to Jerry, "Ann's been hurt," and then darted into the office.

Jerry, still in his swimming trunks, ran over to the office. By the time he got there Dick was telling Carl the details.

"What happened? What happened?" Jerry tried to get Dick's attention.

"Never mind now, just go get some clothes on so that you can go back with us," Dick said.

"But tell me."

"Get dressed," Dick commanded.

Carl was on the phone calling for an ambulance as Jerry ran to the bunkhouse and pulled a pair of jeans over his wet trunks and a sweat shirt over his head. He was back at the office in a couple of minutes.

Jerry, Dick and Carl got back in the jeep and headed to the scene of the accident. On the way Dick filled Jerry in with the details as he had heard them from Ken. When they arrived, Ann was still lying on the ground, and the nurse was bending over her. But Ann's eyes were open and she was talking to them.

124

"The ambulance should be here soon," Dick told the nurse. Then speaking to Ken, he said, "Somebody had better go up to the main road to guide the ambulance driver into this trail."

"I'll go," Ken said, sounding relieved at having something to do which would take him away.

Jerry dropped down on his knees beside the nurse. His eyes widened at the sight of the blood which was still dripping down the side of Ann's face and into her hair. He reached out and brushed back her hair so that it wouldn't get bloody.

"How badly is she hurt?" he asked in a low voice.

"She seems to be breathing normally," the nurse said. "It's just a bump on the head that seems to have knocked her out for awhile. I don't see any other cuts. We won't know about bones until they get her in for X rays."

Ann opened her eyes and saw him. She smiled and reached out. "It's OK, Jerry. I'll be all right."

"Sure you will, Ann. I know you will," he answered, taking her hand.

It seemed like an eternity to Jerry before the ambulance arrived. Nobody talked much, but when they did they whispered as if someone were sleeping. Jerry would get up and walk around, and then would sit down again on the ground and look directly into Ann's face.

The ambulance came, and the nurse got into the seat beside the driver. Carl and the boys went back to the ranch so that Carl could get his car. Both Jerry and Ken asked to go along, but he assured them that there was nothing they could do. There were other guests who needed their attention. So Carl and Ann's parents went into town, and everyone else stayed back at the ranch.

13

Setting Things Right

IT WAS LATE IN THE AFTERNOON when Jerry and Dick took the jeep and went back to the stagecoach to see if they could patch it together enough to bring it back to the ranch. Ken complained of a stiff back and said he would lie down a little while.

They had started to examine the coach when Dick said, "Jerry, come here."

"What's the matter?"

"Look at this broken cable," he said, handing the ends to Jerry. "What do you make of it?"

Jerry frowned in disbelief. "Somebody's cut it!"

"I wondered how it could have broken so casily," Dick said.

"But who?"

"It would have to be someone who was either

crazy, or was deliberately trying to kill Ken," Dick said.

"But why would anyone want to hurt him?"

"He doesn't have any enemies that I know of," Dick responded. "Of course, you haven't been too happy with him lately."

"Whoa, just a minute. You don't think . . . ?"

"I didn't say that I thought anything," Dick interrupted. "I merely suggested that you probably weren't too happy with him. After all, he was riding with your girl."

Jerry became thoughtful. "Do you realize that you're accusing me of something that could easily have been murder?"

"I don't want to believe it," Dick said, "but just the same, we should show this to Carl tomorrow before we move it."

Dick drove the jeep back to the ranch, but Jerry decided to walk. He needed time to think. As he walked questions kept racing through his mind. Who could have done it? Who was that angry with Ken? What would happen when Ken found out about the cable?

He had looked forward to a summer of relaxation and fun, and now look at it. Ken was mad at him. His old girl would probably never go with him again. And Dick had intimated that he had been responsible for the accident. Unless he could find out who did it, he might be accused of attempted murder.

As he saw it, a lot of his troubles started when he had taken Jan away from Ken. "And let's face it," he thought. "I didn't just do it because she was pretty. Ann is just as pretty, and a lot nicer. I did it just to prove I could."

As he walked he decided that if that was the root of the problem, he would have to take care of it. He would tell Jan exactly how he felt, and then Ken would have to take it from there.

When he got back to the ranch, everyone was in the dining hall eating supper. He didn't feel like eating, so he went to the bunkhouse.

He kicked off his boots, and was about to lie down on his bed when he noticed a note on his desk. He picked it up and read:

Jerry:

I had hoped we would become better friends this summer, but now it's all over. You took away the one girl I really wanted, and now you've done something that could have hurt a lot of people just because I was with Ann. Someday you'll learn you can't have everything. I'm going home. You'll have to explain it to Carl, and you'll have to get home the best way you can.

Ken

Jerry stared at the note in disbelief. Then Ken had seen the cut cable, and he did think he had done it.

Jerry dropped his head in his hands. He hadn't cried for years, but now he could feel hot tears dripping from between his fingers and onto his jeans. It seemed as if all the pent-up feelings of the summer came to the surface.

When he finally calmed down, he went into the bathroom and wiped his face. Then he went back to the bed and lay on his stomach with his head buried in his pillow.

Once again, as on so many other occasions that summer, his mind went to Christ. He tried to pray, but this time he couldn't even make sentences. "Lord . . . Lord," he tried. "Help me. You . . . I . . . What do I do now?"

He was still trying to pray when he heard a knock at the door. "Jerry?" It was Jan.

He sat up and tried to wipe his eyes.

"Jerry, are you there?" Jan called again. Now he could hear that she was crying too.

"Come in," he called, "the door is unlocked."

Jan came in. Her eyes were red from crying. Jerry wondered if she noticed his eyes.

Jan sat down on Ken's bed, and started to nervously shred a tissue which she was carrying.

"Jan, what's the matter?" Jerry said, going over and sitting beside her.

"Oh, Jerry, I . . . I . . . ," and she broke out in sobs.

"You what?" Jerry asked, putting his arm around her.

"I . . . I'm so terrible. I should kill myself," she sobbed.

"I don't understand."

"Jerry . . . I . . . I almost killed Ken."

"You?"

"Yes, I caused that accident."

"You? Why?"

"I know it's complicated. I don't know if I can explain it to you or anyone. I'm not sure myself." She blew her nose. "I just couldn't see him running after Ann. I got so jealous that I had to do something. I only wanted to make the coach break down so that she couldn't ride with him. I didn't think they could even get off the grounds with the cable cut like that. You've got to believe me, Jerry! I never thought he'd really take the stagecoach out!"

"You crazy girl. You could have killed them all."

"I know that now, and that's what's so terrible. How can I ever explain this? How can I ever live this down? How can I ever face Ken again?"

"You may not have to," Jerry said, reaching over and picking up the note. "Here, read this."

Jan began to read, and then she started to cry again. "That makes it even worse," she said. "He's blaming you, and you didn't have anything to do with it. Oh, Jerry, I'm sorry. I tried to believe I really liked you, but deep down I knew

I was just using you. I wanted to make Ken jealous, and look at the mess I got myself into. Can you ever forgive me?"

Jerry had gone back to his bed, and was sitting facing Jan. For a long minute, he rested his head in his hands. Then he looked up. "I forgive you, Jan, you know that. And I need to ask your forgiveness. I'm afraid I used you too, just to prove to myself what a great lady's man I am."

"I guess that inside I knew all along what we were both doing and why," Jan said.

Jerry was thoughtful for a moment. "But how about God?" he said. "I think we need to ask His forgiveness, too."

"God? What's He got to do with this?" Jan stiffened.

"Everything. Jealousy and pride caused this whole thing, and that isn't just sinning against each other or Ken; it's against God."

"I never thought of it that way. I didn't think God was much interested in my little likes or dislikes."

"Well, Jan, I just became a Christian this summer, and I've got a lot to learn, but I do know that God will forgive us if we ask Him. That's why Christ died. I think we both played a dirty deal on Ken this summer, and we both need to ask his forgiveness, but first we've got to ask God to forgive us. How about both of us praying?"

"I'll try, but I'm not sure I can," Jan said.

"I'll begin," Jerry said. He bowed his head and began, "Lord. There's a lot I don't know about You, but I do know that You have promised to forgive us when we sin. Thank You for Jesus Christ, and His sacrifice for us. Help us to make it right with Ken."

Then Jan prayed. "I guess I've been a pretty disobedient child. I'm not even sure I am Your child, or that You even want me. But . . . Lord, if You do forgive sin, and You do want me, I want You, and I want Your forgiveness. Please, Lord, help me make this up to Ken and Jerry. I used them both, Lord. Please forgive me. I pray this in Jesus' name. Amen."

They looked up, and for the first time Jan smiled. Jerry smiled back at her. "Now, what about Ken?"

"He's gone, what can we do?"

Jerry looked at his watch. "I wonder if we still can't find him. He's only been gone for about an hour, and I can't imagine that he would go through town without stopping at the hospital. Come on, let's go!"

He grabbed Jan's hand and literally dragged her behind him. They ran out to the jeep, and jumped into it without asking anyone. Jerry drove as fast as the old jeep would go on the way to town. Neither of them spoke the whole way.

When they got to town, he drove immediately

to the hospital, and just as he had predicted, Ken's car was parked in front. They parked beside it and waited.

They had only been there a little while when Ken came out. As he approached his car he saw them. "So, why are you two here?" he asked without smiling.

"We've got to talk to you," Jerry said.

"I can't see that we have anything to talk about. We tried that before," Ken said, opening his car door.

"Wait!" Jerry said, jumping out of the jeep and blocking Ken's way into the car. "This time you've got to listen to us. Jan has something to tell you."

"Do we have to talk here in the street?"

"This is as good a place as any."

"Let's at least get out of town," Ken said.

"How about that turnoff a little way out of town," Jerry answered.

"I'll follow you there."

"No, we'll follow you. I'm afraid you won't come."

"You don't trust me? I'm the one who shouldn't be trusting you."

They drove back toward the ranch, and stopped at the turnoff. Ken parked his car, and Jerry pulled the jeep beside it. They all got out and went to the edge where they could look out over the valley.

"So, what is it you have to say?" Ken asked.

Jan sat down beside Ken on the stone wall, and began her story. She told how she had gone with Jerry all summer thinking it would make Ken jealous, then she told how jealous she had become when Ken spent so much time with Ann. Finally, she told him about the accident.

Ken sat through all of this motionless, looking out over the valley.

"So, Jerry and I have prayed about it, and asked God's forgiveness," she concluded.

"You what?"

"Jerry showed me that Christ could forgive my sin. Now will you forgive me?"

Ken looked over to Jerry. "I've been wanting to talk to you about God all summer, but it doesn't look as if I need to now."

"That's all right. Pastor Mac and I had a good talk that night when he brought me home. I gave my life to Christ then. In fact, it was right here on this very spot. I don't know what I would have done without Christ this summer," Jerry said. "And on a day like this a fellow really needs a friend."

Ken looked back over the valley. "That first day when we stopped here," Ken said, "I prayed that you would find Christ this summer in this valley. He has answered my prayer, but certainly not because of me. I sure messed it up. You've become a Christian in spite of me."

Jerry smiled. Then he saw Ken look at Jan. "Say," he said, "you two have more things to talk about. I think I'll go back to the hospital as long as I'm this close to town. Think Ann will see me?"

"She asked me when you were coming," Ken said.

"That's great." Jerry got in the jeep. "See you back at the ranch," he called as he gunned the motor.

As he started down the road, be looked back to wave at Ken and Jan, but they weren't looking at him.

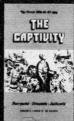